The Return :

Friday morning at 9.30 AM at her house. That was the date agreed for her first spanking in over twenty years. Twenty long years in which, whilst experiencing not so much as a playful swat, she had continued to fantasize and dream of spanking scenarios. These often included being spanked by a range of A list actors, celebrities, characters from fiction, sportsmen or simply reliving more halcyon times when spanking had formed part of her romantic relationship with a loved one.

Twenty years, it was like looking back through history with the wrong end of a telescope. No matter how hard she tried to recall specifics to relive in detail, she only achieved a sense of what had taken place. Searching with the pinprick of memory light for detail, all she could muster were vague thoughts and feelings, all of them positive and hugged to her like a favourite jumper, wrapping her closely in warm comfort. These memories were treasures if ill defined now through the years. They were a backdrop of pleasant fulfilling beats in time, a period of carefree relationship, of experimentation and exploration, of growth, a time before long term commitment and grown up cares. Viewed this way with rose tinted spectacles she'd often thought these memories were rather dangerous placed precariously on a pedestal of remembered enjoyment and passion. They provided solace in times of distress and poor self-esteem but were unchallenged and rooted in emotion rather than fact. Vague echoes of wonder and sensual fulfilment to provide a kernel of dissatisfaction in her vanilla relationship and sexual enjoyment.

Mustn't linger have tidying to complete – on the bed is a pile of washed socks waiting for me to perform the marriage ceremony that will once again unite them. There is a puzzling array of singletons in the group, a result of my daughter's tendency to simply grab the two closest socks regardless of compatibility. A sad looking pile of murky grey soled socks indicate my X-box combatant son's preference for shoeless-ness. Nervous? .... Me?? Surely talking to socks is quite normal in households not hosting a spanking this morning?

Christ! And there in that split second roll back the doubts, the anxieties, the worries. What am I doing and why am I doing it? What if I'm caught doing it? What if I hate it and him? He's a virtual stranger met in a chat room and for a brief live coffee some weeks before. Shortly he is to walk through my front door and we shall engage in activity of the most intimate nature. Too late to back out now he's on his way. Do I want to back out? …………….. No. Taking a calming breath the rising panic sensations are subdued. I've thought this through, decided it is essential to establish whether spanking is as important to me as my continuing fantasizes suggest. This is my opportunity to discover if I want to try and make this part of my life now that I am free to do so.

Keep busy, finish the preparations. You've thought through the logistics many times, coffee, on arrival, taken to the sitting room. Discuss the venue for the spanking to take place. The sofas in the sitting room are old and low, I'm large and heavy we could roll off those and end in an ungainly heap and whilst that might make an amusing anecdote – who could I tell it to? The bedroom then – probably favourite but with a straight backed chair from the dining room brought close to the bed to support my body? I'll see what he thinks of that suggestion. He has said he will not expect me to do anything I'm not happy with. We have discussed my neuroses about my size and exposing myself, he is happy to begin with the time honoured position of over the knee, comfortable, intimate, yet submissive and vulnerable requiring trust between the participants. What had he said about this moment?

"I want you to think about what will happen, I want you to prepare your mind, to allow yourself to blush a little in those quiet moments, to think about the first time you will feel my hand on your bottom, knowing I am looking down at you across my knee a strong hand holding your hip in readiness,

It will be nice, I want you to feel as you have never felt, I want all of the sensations you have ever wanted to wash over you"

I truly hope I can engage with the process and let go of my need to be in control all the time. I would like to relax into the moment and be able to appreciate the myriad sensations and feelings engendered.

He is here. I must hold it together and play the capable hostess, invite him in as though I do this every day. Welcome! a chaste kiss on the cheek for me as we walk to the kitchen for coffee. He is talking generalities I can't attend, I'm flustered and shy. He closes the distance between us and places his hand on my arm. An electric shock pulses through me as I look into his face. He is smiling and talking using quiet words gentling me like a startled horse. He is ushering me up the stairs his hand on my elbow, I feel that what is about to happen is inevitable and unavoidable so maybe now I can relinquish control. He is waiting for me to precede him into the bedroom overtly giving me the choice but nevertheless I feel no doubt as to the outcome.

"A good spanking is all about giving the person you are with the feelings they desire."

He is sitting on the chair and is beckoning me to him with his hand outstretched to mine and now I must commit to him and submit myself into his hands. How did he put it in his most recent mail?

"If by your will you offer your bottom up to be spanked, it is the greatest gift a man could get. It is his duty to treat it tenderly."

I position myself over his lap. He adjusts my position and I feel his hand rest on the cotton of my panties. He smooths the fabric and begins to circle his hand moving over the whole surface. I imagine him looking down at me I feel a little blush creep on my cheeks as I wait for his hand, taking short breaths and waiting, the anticipation almost palpable. He's talking to me, praising my bottom telling me how much he has looked forward to this moment and how much enjoyment we are both about to experience. Mesmerised by his voice I'm focussed on his speech when the first slap is felt. Softly to begin with interspersed with soothing rubs from his palm I begin to breathe again as he creates a gentle rhythm and accustoms me to the feel of his hand. It is at the moment when I begin to relax and breathe regularly and deeply again that I hear him tell me he is going to remove my panties.

A tingling sensation rises from my tummy and I wait for the moment when he lifts the elastic of my panties clear off my back and I feel a cool draft of air on my bottom. I know that at any moment he is going to see a part of me that I keep hidden from all and yet he is a stranger. On the one hand I feel deeply sexual on the other a vulnerable little girl.

The role of women in modern life often doesn't allow for feelings of vulnerability, you are expected to cope with everything by yourself but this little ritual forces you to let go for a while, and maybe release some of the pent up troubles of being a modern woman, setting them aside whilst in these strange but safe hands. We both of us know it's not real, but for an hour or two we let more instinctive feelings take precedence.

As the spanking progresses I retreat deep inside myself, in a way, offering him my vulnerability and because he takes charge, I can let go. The physical sensations combine with feelings. I can feel him focussing on me closely, sensing my responses as I am completely silent. For a time I am so completely lost in my own head that the only thing I know of the outside world is the touch of his hand on my skin.

He draws the spanking to a close. I have experienced intense physical sensations contrasted with highly erotic and sensual caresses of the hot buttocks. The ebb and flow of the spanking rhythm took on a life of its own, there is some discomfort in the sting and burn of the heat in those cheeks but it is not at all unpleasant. I have the feeling that all the troubles of the real world have lifted for this short while that I had surrendered into someone else's care. I feel ………… cherished and wonder what I've done to deserve this oasis of pleasure.

Stephen P. Webb - Spring 2018

The Percussionist :

Chapter 1 :

The card in the shop window read: **"Cleaner required for sound studio 3 nights per week. 6 – 8pm."**

Ellen noted down the contact details for a Rocky Robertson and decided to make contact after work. She needed to earn extra money and this could be an opportunity for her only minutes away from home. It was only six hours per week granted, but it could perhaps open up other opportunities.

Reflecting on her need for more money Ellen's mind returned to the conversations she'd had with her father's solicitor. It was now eighteen months since her father had died of a massive stroke, whilst in the process of firing a junior colleague.

Ellen sighed – just like him to die in the middle of an unkind act, she thought.

She knew, by now, she should be moving on with her life, getting past all the bitterness and disappointment she felt but it was like something had closed down inside her, like the lid on a box. This box held captive all her positive character traits along with all her hopes and wishes for herself and her future life.

It had taken her several months of counselling to recognise this much but she still wasn't making progress towards opening that box and setting her feelings free.

Ellen felt the ever present knot in her stomach tighten a notch and set off the hot gnawing pain which accompanied any prolonged consideration of all her father had done. It seemed to her that all her anger, torment and hurt had been driven inside and had taken root in the core of her being, where it seethed and smouldered, festering and swelling, ever ready to surge up and disgorge a lava-like river of anguish, misery and grief.

James Denton, the Probate Solicitor, had dealt with all her father's affairs and estate – or should that be debts. It seemed Ellen's father had only been a few jumps ahead of the law when he died. He was being investigated for fraud and embezzlement of company funds. He had also run up debts with many local tradesmen and small companies who serviced and supplied his printing works.

The end result had been that instead of inheriting her late mother's family farm, a profitable printing business and the benefits of her father's life assurance policy, she had instead inherited his debts. Debts, bad feeling and infinitely worse, the knowledge that her father had acted in this vile dishonest way showing none of the integrity she had always respected him for.

It was like having her father taken from her twice over. The man she thought she knew and had loved with that special father / daughter bond had gone and now her memories of him had proved to be a mirage, a creation of smoke and mirrors. She could no longer trust her own feelings or reflections where they touched on her memories of him.

The reality she had had to face was that he had been a user, he'd used everything up. He'd re-mortgaged his business premises, her mother's family home and farm and he'd borrowed from anyone who would lend him money - credit cards, personal loans and even friends to the tune of several hundred thousand pounds.

Over the course of the last eighteen months the solicitor had discovered why her father had needed to turn all his assets and more, into cash. He had been gambling at casinos both in London, and on line, and he had been steadily losing.

James Denton had resolved many of the larger debts by selling the business, her father's flat and the family house and farm. These had mainly covered the mortgages and repaid the sums embezzled from the business, and at least allowed that to be sold as a going concern.

Using the proceeds of her father's life assurance policy, Ellen had satisfied the outstanding debts from smaller companies and friends –and in particular, those who needed repayment most urgently. In order to make a comprehensive list of debtors she had had to trawl through boxes and boxes of mail, bills and letters, some begging for restitution. The feelings this engendered, even although she was looking back from the distance of a year and a half, caused that medicine ball of negativity lodged permanently in her gut to stir. It had become more inert over time, but it still billowed and raged given very little encouragement.

Chapter 2

Ellen worked for a theatrical costume designer. It was a job she had enjoyed, but as time went by she found less and less satisfaction from it. She was surrounded by creative people but her role was that of personal assistant to the designer, an elegant title for what in fact was just a 'gopher' as in 'go for this' and 'go for that'. She rarely was called on to release her own creative drive.

The reason she stayed was for the security of a familiar job and a regular salary. There was also the fact that she felt comfortable working beside the same group of faces. She enjoyed largely superficial relationships with them, but she was glad at least, she didn't have to face individuals with dark secrets or destructive, hidden selves.

Ellen had also accepted that it would take her a few more years to pay off all her father's debts and she had resolved to find extra work to hasten the process to a conclusion.

Fifteen minutes after putting down the telephone after the briefest of conversations, Ellen was pushing open the door to Rocky Robertson's sound studio. She wondered about his name, refusing to believe that anyone, in the UK any way, could be christened 'Rocky'. She guessed that it was likely to be a stage rather than his real name and for a brief second she wondered what had made him choose that particular name.

She typed in his name into Google and discovered that Rocky did indeed exist and appeared to have played for a number of bands that she had heard of, as well as an even larger number that she hadn't. Apparently he was an exponent of thrash metal, whatever that was, and had made a lucrative career as a musician who preferred to let others take the limelight and more recently as a successful producer. Ellen was intrigued, although she realised that all he was looking for was a part time cleaner for the studio complex, and she was at a point in her life where she would be grateful to get the job.

As she entered the studio premises she was met by Julie, Rocky's Personal Assistant. She showed Ellen round the building pointing out what her duties would be. It wasn't an extensive area. There were two offices, the reception, a small kitchen and shower room. The majority of space was given over to the recording suite. Julie made her apologies at this point saying that Rocky would be along to take over the interview and explain what she would need to do in the recording area.

Julie left with a cheery "Good Bye then" and Ellen was left in sole possession of the room. She looked around rather aimlessly, feeling a bit like a dog left by its owner and waiting for collection outside a shop.

Ellen looked around the walls of the room which were dominated by a series of large photographs of musicians and bands. She congratulated herself on being able to name a large number of the bands and musicians in the photographs and recognised a number of them that she knew she enjoyed herself. In fact, so engrossed was she in contemplating a particularly colourful shot of a band she liked, in full performance mode that she failed to notice that she was in fact under observation.

Rocky Robertson had quietly entered the Reception area from his studio. He looked over at the young woman waiting to see him, wishing again that he didn't have to employ anyone to clean up. He loathed having anyone fiddling about around him and was especially fierce when it came to non-musicians anywhere near his precious recording equipment.

He had expected Julie to do whatever he needed cleaning wise but when she had rebelled, and refused to pick up a duster or push round the vacuum, and had threatened to resign, he felt he had no other option but to employ a cleaner. Julie was too valuable to him as a PA and a protective, defensive shield against those people he didn't want to talk to. Aside from which, she accepted his little nuances and idiosyncrasies, and also as importantly to Rocky, his unique form of company disciplinary procedure.

Rocky moved forward, making a noise as he did so, and with a bad grace that he appeared to almost snarl said:

"Ellen Moffat?"

Ellen, taken completely by surprise on hearing her name, swung around to face her potential employer. Standing in front of her was a stereotypical example of the older rock star gone to seed. Rocky Robertson had bleached blonde hair, spiked up to an extent that from a distance it looked as if he was wearing a crown. His hair line had receded to an extent and Ellen's first impressions were that it would have benefited from a session with some shampoo for greasy hair.

He was dressed in the uniform of the sessional musician. Faded jeans abundantly ripped and worn together with an anonymous grey coloured, washed out Queens Of The Stone Age T shirt.

His face sported several days' growth of beard and failed miserably to inspire the idea of fashionable stubble. Ellen's eyes were drawn to the tattoos creeping up from his arms and neck towards ear and forehead. Without actually staring Ellen couldn't make out their subject but they seemed to incorporate the many studs and hoops embellishing his lobes and eyebrows.

It was clear to Ellen that this guy spent most of his time in his studio and very little in a gym. His belly overhung the waistband of his jeans by some few inches and his skin beneath the tattoos, stubble and armoured piercings was an unhealthy pasty colour. 'Too much fast food and alcohol' Ellen judged critically.

"Well, are you Ellen Moffat" he growled with a touch of asperity.

Ellen realised after a few seconds that he'd been talking to her and that she'd failed to answer. "Y..y..yes" she stuttered.

"Alright well let's get this over with. Come through to the studio and I'll show you what I need." Rocky replied.

She followed him through double glass panelled doors, into what looked like a control room. Ranked in front of a wall made entirely of glass were myriad rows of electronic mixing decks, recording equipment and computers. As the door closed behind them Ellen became aware of a space empty of sound. Her ears straining to hear anything. Looking upwards she could see acoustic tiling adorned the ceiling and walls, and she realised this was a completely sound proofed room. As she moved further into the room, she glanced through the glass wall to the studio beyond, where she could see a larger space surrounded by the same acoustic tiles.

Attracting her attention again, with that same forceful baritone voice, Rocky began :

"You'll be expected to clean the floors but there's not to be any buckets of water or liquid detergents or cleaners in either studio. The bucket stays in the hall and you go out there to rinse the mop. All of the bins will need emptying and I would expect you to tidy away and wash any coffee cups and that sort of thing. You'll also clean the glass wall and dust the surfaces.

NEVER touch any of the equipment in here, and when there are instruments set up in the studio you're not to touch them either. Have you got that" he barked.

"Clean surfaces, floors, glass wall, empty bins, clear away rubbish and DON'T TOUCH anything. That right?" she retorted, unimpressed with her new boss' social skills.

"Yea, any questions?" he looked at her with suspicion. He wasn't sure but suspected for a minute that she could be taking the mickey.

"You want me to come for 2 hours on Monday, Wednesday and Friday?" she queried.

"Yea, you tidy the reception area and clean round in the kitchen and shower room every day. On Mondays you do out the offices, Wednesday, the recording suite and Friday, the studio. There will be a trial period of a month and once that is over, providing your work is up to my standards, the job is yours for as long as you want it. The pay is £12 an hour" He looked up to see her response and seeing her nod, he went on to agree that she should start tomorrow. He then took her through to see Julie again, who took her personal details and had her sign a contract.

On her way home, Ellen thought that her new boss was unlikely to win any Mr Personality prizes but then again, she was unlikely to see that much of him given her hours of work.

Chapter 3 :

Arriving at the studios on Wednesday night, Ellen could see she might have to revise her opinion of how often she would see Rocky. It seemed musicians didn't work on a 9 -5 kind of schedule and Rocky looked as if he had been at the studio for hours, if not days. During her first hour of work she was aware of considerable traffic back and forth in the studio and being a Wednesday she was aware that she should be cleaning the recording suite. She knocked on the studio but receiving no acknowledgement from anyone, headed in. Rocky was not there but she could see him through the glass wall in the studio.

In complete contrast to its barren state on her last visit, Ellen was amazed to see an extraordinary collection of instruments. Some of the instruments were being erected as she watched, and others were being brought in from a large van at the front door.

Rocky and another man were carrying what looked to Ellen to be an enormous table but she could make out a range of tubes protruding beneath the table top. They set it down next to a bench which already held three instruments that resembled a xylophone.

The instruments were being arranged in a large arc across the studio floor and on the opposite side of the arc to the "table thing" were two enormous round drums and next to them, were what seemed to be two brightly coloured barrels.

Not wanting to be caught goggling through the window Ellen made a start on the cleaning. She was occasionally aware of movement next door but could hear nothing. When she had finished for the night she put away her cleaning tools and quietly left.

Ellen was aware of a sense of anticipation over the next two days. She was really hoping that all those instruments would still be lying around the studio and that she would be able to get a better look at them as she cleaned.

She was aware that never having learned to play an instrument, Ellen was pretty uninformed when it came to identifying orchestral percussion instruments. Her only experience had been at primary school when she got to bang away on chime bars occasionally, and beat time with wooden claves. She had never seen or was able to even name, most of the instruments which met her eyes that night.

The studio seemed deserted by the time she was ready to clean, so she was able to assuage her curiosity to some extent. Carefully cleaning around each instrument stand, she took in the texture of the woods from which many of them were created. She was gazing in fascination at the table like instrument when her heart leaped into her mouth.

"It's called a Marimba".

Ellen spun round with such a guilty expression on her face, that the owner of the voice laughed at her.

Damn this sound proofing, she thought. "I... I'm sorry." She stammered. "I haven't touched any of them."

"Touching is the only way to make my babies sing". The Percussionist closed the door and walked up to Ellen.

"Alan Jones or Jones the drum" he said in a mock Welsh accent. "It's a long time since I've rattled my Cabasa in the Valley's". As he spoke he picked up a wooden instrument which had rows of metal beads around a central pod with a turning handle and serrated edge. When he twisted it the shaker made some really funky rhythms.

"I'm Ellen the cleaner" she said with quiet humour.

"Well Ellen the Cleaner, he quipped, let me introduce you to my family"

Taking her hand he walked over to the Marimba. She could now see that laid across the table like structure, were a series of tuned wooden bars. These were suspended over tubular resonators which reached down in differing lengths towards the floor. Alan ran his hand over the wooden blocks which were a golden honey colour. He picked up a stick, which he told her was called a beater, and began to pick out an upbeat tune with a calypso rhythm. The beater had a soft end and as a result, the music he drew from the wooden bars was muted and mellow.

They moved across to a table set to the side of the marimba and here were xylophones and glockenspiel. Taking four beaters in his hands he played a little riff on them. He explained that these were all pitched instruments and he demonstrated how he changed their tone and sounds, by using various beaters made of wood and rubber.

Next, he ushered her over to the huge Timpani drums at the centre of his arc. He described to Ellen how to tune the skins which were stretched over enormous copper bowls, that could be adjusted by cranking metal keys situated around the rim. He showed her how the foot pedal could be used to dampen the sound and the subtle variations in tone that different beaters could produce.

They were surrounded by a mass of different drums. The colourful barrels were hand drums from Latin America and he played her a wild few bars of hand drumming in the Sabar tradition. He pointed out a snare drum and something called Roto Toms, which seemed to be different sized drums tuned to individual notes. There were also cymbals, triangles and bells of all sizes hanging from a metal frame.

By this time she was totally captivated, entranced by the passionate, almost fanatical, enthusiasm that spilled from Alan Jones. He emanated a childlike joy as he caressed and held his precious instruments intoning the exotic names so new and unknown to Ellen. By now she was bemused by a superfluity of new information, as the names flowed away from her intriguing her with their unfamiliarity - Guiro, Castanets, Vibra slap, Celesta. Alan passed them over to her to try and she enjoyed the way they sounded and felt on her tongue.

Curiously, Ellen surreptitiously studied Alan. He was taller than her, but she couldn't really gauge his true height as he stood with stooped posture and concave chest, as though he was so used to bending forward he could no longer straighten up. His hair was a very light auburn colour which Ellen knew some confidently would call strawberry blonde. His largely nondescript facial features were redeemed by a pleasant smile which extended whenever he placed his hands on an instrument or described to Ellen, how the instrument was played. She mused that he was far from the image of the dashing and impressive musicians she'd had in mind when starting the job.

Despite it being well after her finishing time, Ellen felt compelled to stay and listen to Alan in the same way a moth is drawn to a light in darkness. He had seemed to forget all about her presence as he moved from instrument to instrument playing short phrases of music. Unobserved, outside of the spotlight illuminating the arc of the instruments, she watched him.

As he became more absorbed by his music, he seemed to flow from one piece to another and Ellen was struck by the beauty of his hands. Until now she had consigned him to her mental category of nondescript, ordinary looking and poorly dressed musician with no particularly outstanding features. Now however, she became aware of his hands.

They were shapely with long expressive fingers. She loved the way he held them when he beat the drums. She could see he formed different shapes with them, sometimes cupping air in the palm, sometimes striking with flat hard palm, sometimes finger flicks and sometimes gentle pats. His hand causing resonance changes on the drum which he varied, to accentuate the rhythms.

As he beat a pulsating, dynamic, repeating rhythm, Ellen began to feel her body responding. There was something visceral about the music and it seemed to be finding an answering pulse from her heartbeat. The crescendo of sound built up, until the power of that beat was all she could feel, as if every other thought had been suppressed by this elemental fusion of tempo, sensation and rhythm.

She found her breathing was accommodating to the voice of the drums and as the drumming continued she found herself, moving, swaying and nodding in time to the beat. It was liberating, she felt as if she was being drawn evermore deeply into the heart of the music and outside of herself.

Then with a suddenness which ripped a cry of loss from her throat the drumming ceased. Alan looked up startled, he had zoned out, inhabiting that place where musicians go to commune with their art, and for a few moments he had no concept of where he was or who had cried, as though her very breath was being torn from her body.

Before he could speak to her, Ellen had slipped away through the door desperate to escape further notice. She had no idea what had happened to her in there and she needed the safety of her familiar little flat in which to explore these sensations. Her pulse rate was soaring and her whole body felt wired and tingly. She'd never experienced such an immediate, intimate and physical reaction to anything like that before.

From the darkened recording suite, Rocky Robertson had watched Ellen's capitulation to the primal rhythms of the percussion. He observed with growing fascination, the rapid succession of changing expressions as they flowed across her face. He noted the tumult of emotions exposed in those fleeting moments, allowing a glimpse of the hidden Ellen and felt he could see a complex and deeply troubled individual. In those few minutes, he had seen behind her usually strictly schooled features and guarded expressions. For reasons he could not yet identify, he felt compelled and moved to get to know her better and if necessary to help her.

Chapter 4 :

Over the course of the next two weeks Alan remained at the studio. By day he recorded various percussion backing tracks which were mainly for a number of commercials. During the evenings however, he gave full rein to his passion, rehearsing with absolute and total concentration the Percussion Concerto.

Drawn to listen to Alan's music with a desire she could not explain, Ellen stayed behind after her shift every evening, listening enthralled to the range of sounds Alan could create and the sensations they inspired in her.

She could think about little else, she was distracted during her day at work and for the last few nights, she had also dreamed of the Percussionist and his wonderfully talented hands.

This evening, carefully cleaning around him in the studio, she caught herself daydreaming about the hypnotic movement of those hands as he caressed the surface of the drum skins, and how he gently drew his fingertips across the Guido, rippling his finger ends along the indented surface.

She shivered as in her imagination she felt the touch of his fingers transferred to her body. Instead of waves of vibration palpating the drum, it was her skin that quivered, shimmering as he strummed. The image in her mind's eye was of her naked form stretched before the maestro's hands. She writhed as they flittered over the delicate skin of her naked breasts vacillating between soft feather light touches and spasms of rapping, smarting, stinging slaps tormenting the flesh. She envisioned his hands playing over the surface of her back his fingertips smoothing their passage over her taut buttocks. She sighed as she conjured the exquisite sensation of his elegant hands fondling and soothing, then squeezing and grazing the valley of her thighs.

Her heartbeat hitched with excitement, when his hands reached out and clasped heavy beaters bringing them down on her buttocks with a clangourous slap causing pulsating, reverberating tremors of sound. Her breath exploded from her as his hand suddenly delivered a series of staccato beats, little sharp taps, harder strokes, a throbbing beat, stridently building to a thunderous resounding, stentorian crescendo, a shock wave of sensation and sound.

Chapter 5 :

As the days progressed Rocky continued to watch Ellen. He was charmed by her naive fascination with the percussion instruments and was moved by the transformation in her face as she gave herself over to the music and elemental rhythms.

These past two nights he had observed a change in her. She seemed more distant, quieter than ever. He had not heard her humming the little melody which usually placed her in the building. It was a sweet tune he couldn't identify at first, he wasn't even sure that she was aware of humming it. After her first couple of sessions he had tried playing the key phrases on his guitar and let his subconscious fill in the gaps. He realised it was "Vincent" by Don McLean a ballad about the life and death of Vincent Van Gogh. What was the significance of that for Ellen he wondered?

Tonight as she listened to the music, Rocky felt a wisp of relief as mounting excitation lightened her mood. He still saw flashes of the darker emotions he sometimes read on her face, when concentrating on the undemanding cleaning tasks that she performed for him, sadness, anguish, hurt, an awful raw anger and disappointment. Tonight, however, they were swiftly followed by fascination, longing, desire and yes, arousal.

As she became more entranced by the music, he could see a physical increase in her rate of breathing, her face was flushed and her eyes bright and unfocussed. She was quivering like a bow string poised for release.

Now more than ever, Rocky wanted to help Ellen. He thought it was ironic that she had never been less aware of him and his presence than in the last two evenings and yet he felt drawn ever more closely to her. He sensed her burden. He could feel the weight he thought caused by suppressing and concealing troubled feelings.

Pondering her obvious response to the music and judging by her profound need for release, he began to have an idea of a way in which he might be able to help.

He would wait for an opportunity to present itself.

Chapter 6 :

The two weeks of the percussion recordings were complete and all of the instruments had been packed away and were now being transported to

Birmingham where Alan was scheduled to perform the Percussion Concerto.

Entering the studio for the first time since it had been emptied, Ellen stood looking forlornly around. She was experiencing an immense sense of loss, but also a deep seated frustration, as though she couldn't complete any of the tasks she started. She moved very slowly through her cleaning tasks, her face and her body a picture of complete dejection.

Rocky watched her, sensing and tasting her confusion and resentment, and thought he wouldn't need to wait much longer before he would act.

The following night Ellen couldn't see anyone in the building as she commenced her work and believing the studio to be deserted she went into the recording suite. Up until this point she had been almost obsessively adhering to all Rocky's rules concerning his studio equipment. She had avoided touching, or getting in close proximity to anything, except for the instruments Alan had passed over to her during their first meeting.

Tonight however, she was moved to disobey. She needed to hear the music. She was compelled to relive those beats, to recapture the feelings and to allow the rhythms to enter her and lift her, as before. She had felt something other than pain and sorrow when the music played and she wanted to recapture those emotions.

She had only just found the CD she had been looking for and popped it into the player when Rocky returned. He had returned to the studio to pick up some sheet music and he saw Ellen in the control room. He couldn't hear anything, but judging by the movements of her body and her sensuous, undulating swaying, she was listening to a track from Alan's music. This was the opportunity he'd been waiting for.

He made his way unseen and unheard back into the recording suite. Ellen's back was to the door and she had not heard him come in. He didn't want to frighten her but he did want to make an impression and wrong foot her. He closed the space between them and spoke her name:

"Ellen"

She flew round squealing as she met Rocky face to face. Shock was followed by a guilty blush across her cheeks, and inadvertently she emitted a long "Oh" on an intake of breath.

"Ellen" Rocky repeated. "Have you used my equipment?"

She couldn't speak and just nodded her head, shooting her gaze down towards the floor.

"Ellen?" Rocky persisted trying to make eye contact with her.

Stammering and darting anxious glances between the recording deck and the door she nodded again and said

"I'm s- s- s- sorry. I just needed to hear it again. I'm sorry I touched your stuff." She began to cry softly.

Feeling unbelievably touched, Rocky very gently asked,

"May I have your hand?"

Ellen's moved her gaze upwards towards his and her face and body language asked her question without the need for anything to be said.

"May I have your hand?" Rocky repeated with a small smile.

With no understanding of why she felt obliged to comply Ellen offered her left hand to Rocky. He took it in his extremely large, paw like hand and exerting a gentle pressure he led Ellen from the room.

He guided her from the building and accompanied her on the short walk to her home, all the while holding her hand safely in his.

Ellen followed in stunned silence. She had no desire to remove her hand, no curiosity as to where they were going or the reasons why. Her entire concentration was focussed on the sensory receptors within her hand and the knowledge that she had given Rocky possession of it.

They arrived at Ellen's flat. She fished out her key and fumbled with it, failing as if intoxicated to get it into the door lock. Rocky offered his hand and Ellen gestured for him to try. Her eyes focussed on the blue and red design of the tattoo covering his hand. The tattoo was of a vine whose tendrils clung to his fingers and climbed across the back of his hand and up his arm. There were little star shaped flowers almost hidden beneath the leaves of the vine. Each flower had an initial on it, which added to the mystery, with Ellen wondering what the initials represented? Ellen found herself imagining names of friends or former lovers whom Rocky had chosen to immortalise in his design.

The door was opened and Rocky followed Ellen inside. Ellen shyly accepted the key, feeling a little frisson of electricity tickle her hand as their palms briefly touched. Rocky also felt it and smiled at her catching her eye, winning a nervous fragile, little smile in return.

Ellen emboldened by this connection offered him a drink. Rocky asked for coffee and whilst she went to make it he looked around the room. It was neat and sparsely furnished. There was a large sofa on which Ellen had arranged a number of cushions, a small coffee table holding a number of books in subjects from Impressionist art to Drummers of the World. There was a small fireplace set with logs ready to be lit, and above the mantelpiece was a large print of Vincent Van Gogh's self- portrait. A little desk under the window completed the ensemble, giving a pleasant sense of light and space within the room.

Ellen brought back mugs of coffee and they sat in companionable silence drinking. Unsure of what he might be expecting, she apologised once again for touching his recording equipment.

"You did break my rules" he said with a shrug. "What is it that you enjoyed so much about the drumming?"

Ellen looked up into his face and tried to conceptualise what it was she had so loved about it. Using her hands to create expressive pictures she said :

"It made me feel……..." She couldn't bring it to the surface enough to label with a single word, but her hands were miming a fountain shape starting low near her stomach and with her palms together, surging up to open out at head level. An image of an erupting volcano venting forth was painted in Rocky's vision.

He smiled, nodding with understanding. Taking her coffee cup from her hand and placing it on the table he caught her gaze and said :

"Will you trust me with your hand again?"

Slowly and hesitantly she placed her left hand in his. She looked at the size differences between their hands and the colour variations of his tattoos where they merged with her very light skin. He placed her hand palm down on his right thigh and covered it with his hand. She was aware of the fabric of his jeans beneath her palm, the warmth of his hand as it sheltered hers beneath it and the gentle caresses of his thumb as he stroked her mound of Venus. She smiled up at him liking the sensation of having, one of her hands in safe keeping.

Moving her hand slightly farther across his lap and causing Ellen to lean closer to him, Rocky gradually closed the gap between them as they sat on the sofa. He gently caressed her as he carefully placed his arm around her shoulders. The fingers of his right hand began to softly brush and stroke her arm. He continued to soothe her with his gentle touch, and slowly, very, very, slowly, millimetre by millimetre, he drew her to him.

Ellen's senses felt as if they were reading a map of her body. Wherever she could feel Rocky's touch, the nerve endings of her skin where firing off multiple bursts of heat. She gradually let her weight merge with his, until her head was resting in the crook of his shoulder. She felt their breathing unify and she absorbed his warm musky scent.

Not wanting her to become too settled Rocky bent his mouth close to her ear and quietly said :

"Will you let me have your other hand?"

After a minutes pause, she placed her right hand in the upturned palm of his left sliding it next to her other hand. Rocky's fingers clasped around them enclosing them in his large fist.

"Do you trust me to keep them safe?" he asked.

Ellen nodded, a rueful smile playing around her lips. She was content to let him hold her, with the rhythm of his caresses on her arm swaying her languidly against his chest. Steadily, almost imperceptibly Rocky eased her shoulders forward, continuing to soothe and reassure her as he drew her to face his lap.

Cautiously he inched her body with delicate even pressure from his arm until she was poised in front of and leaning across his chest. Tenderly he placed her two hands on the far side of his left thigh causing her to stretch further over his lap to the point where with only the smallest relinquishment of control she would lie down on his lap. With infinite patience he waited cosseting her with his easy embrace. Slowly, inexorably she sank down on to him.

Rocky began to rub her back in a tender, sensual massage. His hands circled her body, from her shoulders down to the small of her back. His fingers traced the muscle shapes, lingering to caress and stroke, covering the relief map of her contours. Gingerly at first, he began patting her, tapping his hands over her taut muscles and gradually increasing the tempo, and finding a rhythm which complemented the rise and fall of her ribcage. Little by little, he felt her relinquishing control of her posture, melting into his lap, and absorbing the sensations of his hands moving over the surface of her back.

Without breaking the mood, Rocky whispered to her

"Ellen will you trust me to help you?"

She sighed nodding as she rubbed her head lightly against his thigh. Sliding one arm under her chest, and the other under her thighs, he lifted her, repositioning her body by placing her wholly across his lap with her head and legs resting on either side of him along the sofa.

He recommenced his careful stroking and massaging of her back, but this time extending over the perfectly positioned rise of her bottom. As he gently covered the entire surface of her bottom, he waited for her to once again release control of her muscles and sink in to his lap. With steadily increasing firmness he caressed her bottom kneading the flesh through her thin cotton trousers and periodically delivering a gentle tap with the palm of his hand.

Guardedly, and with careful deliberation, Rocky introduced Ellen to the sensual art of spanking. Rocky hoped that, if Ellen would allow herself to take this journey, she would replicate, even extend, the feeling of release that had begun in the percussion beat and rhythm she had responded to on such a primal level in the studio.

Rocky's hand rose and fell, contacting her bottom with gentle spanks. By varying the speed and intensity of each slap he kept her guessing, never knowing the extent of sensation she would feel. By also deliberately pausing between each spank, he ensured Ellen could feel the warmth generated across her bottom.

Lying completely still across his lap Ellen accepted the spanks as an extension of the massage that had lured her into a quiescent and passive state. She was aware of the increasing force of Rocky's hand which rhythmically rose and fell on her behind. Her flesh had begun by tingling, with almost a tickling sensation, which when his hand rubbed and kneaded the skin, faded only to re-energise as the hand fell again. She was living in the moment between each sharp slap, as she anticipated and accepted the increasing pleasure and desire she was feeling.

The warmth of her buttocks intensified as Rocky maintained a relentless delivery of spanks. She began to vocalise as the sensations which she had found stirring and moving initially, now began to overwhelm her senses. She reacted by arching her back against the hand Rocky rested there. He soothed her, circling his hand in the age old gesture of reassurance, and then whispered to her:

"Let it come, give yourself over to it" he quietly said.

He continued to spank her, with each spank becoming harder now. He concentrated the spanks in groups of three and four consecutive strikes before pausing. As Ellen's distress increased, she became aware of the familiar pressure deep within the core of her, enlarging, swelling, mounting and distending her insides. She began to fight to suppress it, to box it in but with unremitting energy she felt it magnify until with an excruciating intensity she felt it rupture, spewing forth all the rage, bitterness, anguish and grief trapped within her for the last eighteen months.

At this spectacular eruption of pent up emotion, Ellen was wracked by gut wrenching sobs. Her whole body was given over to pitiful and frenzied crying in an uncontrollable out pouring of grief. Her cries pierced Rocky's soul, and he gathered her up in his arms and held her, whilst she cleansed herself of all the negativity that dwelt within her.

He comforted her rocking back and forth making no attempt to stem the release. As he felt the violence of the storm of sobbing and weeping diminish, he whispered gentle words of comfort and softly began humming the melody from "Vincent" into her ear. When she recognised the tune, Ellen grasped Rocky in a tight embrace hanging on to him as if she might otherwise float away. She wept the tears of loss of a daughter for her dearly loved father, the father who used to sing "Vincent" to her to help her sleep at night.

It was some time before Rocky sensed a change in the intensity of her weeping. He mused to himself that he had unwittingly taken the advice of William Shakespeare to "Oppose not rage while rage is in its force, but give it way a while and let it waste".

He would have been surprised to learn that Ellen, searching to understand what she had just experienced, was contemplating two of the sayings her counsellor was fond of quoting:

"Tearless grief bleeds inwardly" and "He that conceals his grief finds no remedy for it."

She had considered them at the time very trite, "fortune cookie" like wisdom. Now though, she thought that perhaps there was some substance to them and when she was again capable of coherent thought, she may open herself up to the possibility of healing.

For now she felt an extraordinary tiredness and couldn't think about anything else tonight. She just felt so very, very tired. She became conscious of the strong arms that held her securely, protecting her from a return of her demons and allowing her to slip into a more peaceful state than she had known in many months. She was also no longer aware of the hot painful ball in her stomach.

Recognising that she was spent, Rocky carried her through to her bedroom, settled her in bed and waited, stroking her hair and humming her song until she surrendered to a deep sleep. He let himself quietly out of the flat, sensing that it would be better for her to wake alone to begin to absorb and process the events of the night before.

He would wait until she was ready to come to him.

Stephen P. Webb - Spring 2018

The Hotel :

He sat on the bed reflecting on all the enjoyable images, sensations and arousal of the last few hours. He had been concerned on the approach to the hotel that he had allowed too long for this their first meeting.

Rafe was a long time spanko, deeply committed to his stable of spankees whom he saw regularly throughout the year. This meeting had been the first with a new spankee and she had been different, much more trouble than all his other regular girls put together. A mass of fears and inhibitions but something about her had attracted him. There was something of the adventurer in his soul and he was intrigued by the possibilities of writing on what presented as a virtually blank slate.

He'd chosen a middle range hotel with comfortable rooms and incurious staff. He was confident and straight forward in his approach and was not a little amused by her obvious discomfort at walking into the hotel lobby. Her face held something of the 'startled rabbit caught in headlights' look and her frequent glances towards the door spoke volumes of the internal battle that raged within her – should she stay or should she leave whilst leaving was still an option?

He had helped to prepare her for this moment by talking her through it and laying out scenarios to try and give her some landmarks to help her navigate by. He had ended by saying that she could of course change her mind at any point - until she was inside the room with him. After that time the inevitability was a spanking on her bare bottom.

The room was empty of her now. She had stayed and they had enjoyed a full encounter, everything he had planned to enthral her as a spider traps a fly. He had spanked her sensuously, raising a glorious hue of elegant crimson shades equitably across her buttocks and thighs. He had gazed at the curves of her buttocks, the shaded valleys of her upper thigh and under buttocks, the smooth dip to the merging of buttock and lumbar spine. He had felt her quiver and thrill to the touch of his hand, caressing, soothing, spanking, shattering her calm, outward control with explosions of flat palmed kisses and restoring equilibrium with fingertip massage and stroking of the, by now, hot pimpled flesh.

He had drunk in the symphony of sounds she'd made ranging from the wisps of sound barely audible as gasps, to the tunefully vocal song as his hand conducted, driving the rhythm, increasing the pace and settling into a steady beat.

She had left minutes before replete and thankful, the possessor of secrets and recipient of his care and skill. Her pleasure in the meeting had been obvious and his was still insistently present, reminding him of the depth of his enjoyment of the day.

Rafe was brought back to the moment by a tentative knocking on the door. Opening it he saw a slight, dark haired beauty in the uniform of the hotel's chambermaid service. She had in her arms some towels and was indicating her intention of bringing them into the room. Rafe studied her as she placed them next to the pile already provided. He recognised her as the maid who had been cleaning rooms along his floor on his arrival that morning.

He continued to watch her as she hesitated to leave, casting furtive glances around the room. Amused by her curiosity, Rafe had a suspicion that his previous encounter had not been as private as he'd thought. Had the maid overheard the spanking symphony in full fortissimo? Well, he pondered, let's find out what she thought of that.

Catching her eye Rafe smiled and said "She's gone" and after a pause, "Are you my next?"

The hazel eyes held his in a hypnotic stare. The plump cherry lips quivered as though trying to find words for a response and enjoying her discomfiture Rafe observed as the colour– his favourite crimson – flooded, delightfully slowly, into her soft feminine cheeks.

He waited her out knowing that he'd not been wrong. She'd understood him only too well. Unable to speak but showing no signs of leaving, the chambermaid produced a fleeting nod of her head. "Well now, that's perfect" Rafe smiled and gently offered her his hand. Still locked in his gaze she tentatively reached out and made contact with her finger tips and stood as the slightest of shivers played up her spine as she processed the sensation of his fingers playing with hers - moving about the landscape of her hand, gradually establishing possession, until his hand completely engulfed hers.

She was nervous and they'd had no discussion, no conversation at all and therefore no possible way to have agreed what was to follow. But here she was and by all the signs she was very definitely expecting to be spanked. Rafe wanted to help her to relax and eventually to speak to him! He drew her carefully to him, requesting, rather than insisting, that she come through light pressure on her hand and an encouraging smile. He gathered her in, gently circling her shoulders with his arms and letting her hide in the warmth of his embrace. Her head lay on his chest and he could feel warm breath coming in little panting waves against his T shirt.

He held her lightly, companionably rather than possessively wanting her to become comfortable with the way their bodies felt together and to welcome, rather than startle to, his touch. As he felt her breathing quieten he spoke to her, "well now, you are still here." She nodded, not looking at him. He lifted her chin with his cool fingers forcing her to face him and once again meet his gaze.

"You know why you are here?" he asked her, measuring the changing size of her eyes as they widened in what? fear? anticipation? desire?

Again she nodded. "And you wish to stay, to continue?" Rafe paused and before she could nod once more his expression halted her and she realised she would have to make an actual spoken response this time.

"I, I want to stay" she blurted out, muttering a plaintive "please" as an after thought.

"And what do you expect to happen now?" Rafe persisted in waiting for her reply, unrelenting, despite her reluctance to speak. She had to ask him to establish her willingness for him to spank her. He could see she was nervous but sensed too her resolve.

All in a rush the words poured out, "I want you to do it like you did for her." She breathed out, the air gushing from her in a whoosh of relief. A momentary respite was all she experienced as Rafe said quietly, "Not good enough I'm afraid you must tell me, explicitly."

The amusement Rafe felt at the look of frustration and pique that sped across her pretty features he was careful not to show and he waited patiently whilst she gathered her determination and courage and spoke more clearly and resonantly than he had so far heard.

Inhaling deeply she began, "I want you…… to s ..s spank me….. like you did….your girlfriend." The answer rocketed out in staccato phrases. Her face shone bright crimson and just as she began to look away from him to absorb the enormity of what she had just requested, Rafe took her left hand and led her to the sofa. He sat her next to him and controlling her left hand he pulled her up and guided her firmly until she was positioned over his lap. He laid his left hand in the small of her back and paused to give her time for her breathing to moderate once again.

His right hand was gently describing circles over her uniform clad bottom, slowly and sensuously smoothing the tight cotton over the shapely curves of her pert rear. He felt more than heard a hitch in her breathing and a little gasp which became a sigh as she relished these new sensations.

Smiling inanely as he remembered just how he had come to be in this enviable position, Rafe quietly whispered in the direction of her ear,

"Now we'll see what eaves dropping will bring you" and with that he began to spank her waiting bottom.

Stephen P. Webb - Spring 2018

The Accountant :

The meeting has been set for 11am next Tuesday morning and as usual you have confirmed that you need me to do some bean counting.

When I arrive, it is obvious that you have forgotten the appointment and that I have taken you back somewhat. I have arrived in my usual professional attire, complete with hair tied back in a bun, glasses and a suit, stereotypical accountant.

From the start of the meeting, it is obvious that you are less than impressed at my arrival and are seriously not in the mood for me. I notice though that you did stare at my legs in my skirt, which I suspect is shorter than you would have expected.

The meeting does not go well. I don't find half the items I think should be there and you're getting more and more frustrated with me. Of course what you don't know is that I've been making you bend over to check things all the time because I like the view and actually I'm really rather enjoying myself. I know you're getting really annoyed with me but that is part of the pleasure of the job. You are required to do what I ask you to and that's fun. I enjoy the power trip.

I tell you that I am going to have to write up a report on your deficiencies. Considering I haven't found a single important thing this is really the last straw. You turn on me and start telling me exactly what you think of me and my report. I'm caught off guard and back away, stuttering about who I am and your requirement to follow my orders. Since you're already going to get into trouble for shouting at me, you decide you might as well get it all off your chest and with me backed against the wall you carry on telling me what you think until you realise that the alarmed look in my eyes is turning you on. You stop.

We stand there looking at each other for a minute or two and I'm curious about the look in your eyes. The anger has gone but I can't tell what it has been replaced with. It looks like you are getting aroused but that seems unlikely. Thinking about it, your proximity and all the testosterone you've been throwing around has actually been turning me on too but I tell myself not to be ridiculous.

Amused at my indecision as to what to say or do, you take me by surprise by coming straight up to me putting your arm round my waist and kissing me hard. I kiss you back, with equal passion, for a few seconds, taken aback by how much I want you until I realise what I'm doing and I push you away. You twist one of my arms behind my back and pull me in to kiss me again.

Again, I respond for a few seconds before stopping myself and I manage to get away and slap you. You twist my arm behind my back too and pull me in hard against you. I struggle to get away but you lock my arms more so I end up pushing against you to try and mitigate the pain. Holding my wrists tight behind me you kiss me again. I realise I cannot get away and wriggle half heartedly, more for the sake of it but feeling even more aroused, kiss you back. Enjoying the response you have been getting you release my wrists and annoyed at myself, I push you back with my new found freedom and slap you again. Annoyed you grab me round the waist and you pull me in for another kiss, temporarily giving in to the desire you're creating.

I realise how absurd this is again and pull away and slap you again. This time I can see that you are becoming annoyed with me for slapping you. There isn't a deal of power behind each slap, to cause damage but I can tell it smarts and is to a degree unnecessary! In the absence of a better idea and because I'm still annoyed with myself, I go to slap you yet again but you catch my hand and twist it back behind me so I'm up on tip toes.

You get very close to my face and tell me to stop slapping you or I might get considerably more than I think I want! You let go of my wrist and grab me pushing me back against the wall. Again, you stretch me up on tip toes to sow me who is the boss and who now is in control. I try to push you off me and hit out again at you, but you are further away than I can reach and I give up very quickly after starting. You relax your grip enough so I can sink back onto my heels and you again kiss me, forcing me hard back against the wall and penetrating my mouth with your tongue. Your kissing me too hard for me to stop you even if I wanted to, which I don't.

The hunger and urgency of your kiss makes me unbelievably aroused and I know I want you to take me right there and then. I feel awful about myself for wanting that but think that perhaps I don't need to worry about it, because I have a suspicion you'll take what you want anyway. My arms go limp at my sides in resignation as to what is happening.

I eye you suspiciously wandering what you will do next. You don't move and are evidently trying to decide the same thing. You take a flick knife from your pocket and open it, amused at the concern in my eyes. This was unexpected! You come over to me and slide the blade down my cheek. Slowly over my throat, turning in the blade just slightly so I get that hint of pain and I wince, carefully so as not to make it worse. You turn the blade on its side again and trace it down in between the open neck of my blouse and then slice through the thread of all the buttons. You pull the blouse free of my skirt and fully open and then run the side of the blade over the outside of my bra on each side before turning the knife onto the blade edge and then running it down my cleavage. The shivers of excitement are unbelievable. You catch my response and slide your hand up my skirt to check and sure enough you feel the moistness already there in the cotton of my panties.

You slide my skirt up so its in folds at my hips, slide the knife behind the material of my underwear and cut them from me. You then take the side of the blade and slide it up my thigh till I can feel the cold metal between my legs. My whole body shivers with excitement. You return the blade to my throat and kiss me again excited at the responses you are getting.

You put the knife to one side and slide your hand back between my legs, this time sliding a finger inside me. I'm incredibly aroused and I feel slide a further finger in and fuck me slowly with them, still probing my mouth with your tongue and your other hand holding me tightly around the waist.

My hips have tilted to get you better access and I'm slowly starting to move against your hand. You leave my mouth to kiss down my throat and between my breasts, your fingers never stopping inside me. I can feel your breath on me and I want your tongue on me too. I try to lean forward so that I'm closer to you, encouraging you to lick me but you push me back against the wall continuing to probe inside my pussy, fucking me with your fingers. After what seems like a torturous age, I finally feel your tongue on me and shockwaves of pleasure race through my body.

You work me relentlessly until I'm on the verge of cumming and then you stop and withdraw your fingers. I cry out in distress much to your amusement. You feed your fingers to me and I suck at them hungrily. You turn me round and push me against the wall. I hear you undoing your trousers and arch back waiting for your cock to finally slide into me, desperate for it. I wait for what seems like an age but nothing happens.

I start to turn round to see where you are and what you're doing but you tell me to stay where I am. All of a sudden there's a crack in the air and I jump trying to look round to see what it is? You tell me to stay still or I will regret it. There's the crack again. What is that? The third crack tells me what it is as I feel the sting on my left bum cheek and then again on the right. It's stingy but not too bad, so apart from yelping in surprise at the first strike I manage not to respond to it. You are mildly surprised that I'm not protesting so you experiment with a further flick of your belt on either side. Still not hard enough to do more than cause some reddening briefly. I flinch each time but nothing more. Deciding that this is an invitation to go harder you flick me again on either side. This produces a much more satisfying sound, but still I do not cry out although you can see the skin quivering in response so you know it's hurting.

You come up to me and rub the skin on both sides whispering into my ear that you think I like the pain and that is probably a good thing because you haven't really got started yet. Just to check that I am enjoying it you slide your fingers back inside me briefly and I immediately arch back onto your hand which gives you your answer and you smile to yourself. You let me clean your fingers again before resuming your position and cracking your belt together to make that satisfying sound. You don't really need to hit me to send shivers of excitement through me, hearing the sound in the air is enough.

You give me a few light strokes again to warm me back up to it but then you build up harder and harder. I'm straining my wrists against the chains to control the pain. Having been here before I know that if I move I'm likely to cause more pain from a mishit than if I stay exactly where I am. My skin is starting to burn and you're getting closer and closer to my pain threshold but still you carry on. At least you're keeping it even so both sides hurt as much as each other. You're at the point of leaving marks now and it's amusing you seeing the belt imprints on either side. You reckon you're probably pushing it and are surprised I haven't stopped you.

Coming up to me again you ask if I have had "enough yet?" I'm struggling to breathe but manage to nod marginally. "Do you think that's your decision to make?" I shake my head as much as I can. You slide your belt from my throat knowing it will burn as it slides away. You step back just far enough to be able to hit me with your hand and you spank me so hard my whole body recoils in pain. Admiring the nice mark you've left you move over to the other side.

Knowing what's coming I try and tell myself not to tense and remind myself how much more that will hurt but at the same time imploring you with my eyes not to do it so hard. But you do anyway and again I recoil in pain, tears stinging my eyes. You stand back to admire your handiwork and notice the tears in my eyes. After a minute or 2 of conjecture about what to do next you ease my skin slightly by rubbing it down to soothe it. I start to relax finally feeling some relief.

You notice my body calming down and decide that you much prefer me to be tense and wound up. I feel your hand move the air and I brace for impact but nothing happens. Perplexed I try to see what's happening but I can't. Then I'm suddenly aware of a piece of material in front of my mouth.

"Open!"

"Wh….." I was trying to ask what it was and why but as soon as my mouth opened it was filled with the material which you tie behind my head. It is uncomfortably tight and digging into the sides of my mouth. I try to protest, fighting with the chains round my hands and trying to turn around wriggling like crazy but you're standing behind me again holding me still.

You slide your hand back between my legs from behind. I'm fairly dry after all the pain and then being gagged unexpectedly, but you work me gently with your fingers to get me wet again. You feel me start to relax and enjoy it, my head tipping back. I hear you opening your trousers once more with your spare hand and wait for fulfilment finally. Sure enough your fingers withdraw and I feel your cock slide into me slowly. I can feel how hard you are and it feels fantastic. I push back against you so I can feel more of you inside me. Your hands slide to my hips briefly for a few hard thrusts before one hand slides round to my clit. You fuck me really slowly knowing I want more than that but you're just teasing me enjoying how wound up you're getting me. You're using your hand on my hip to stop me from pushing back and you can feel me tensing with frustration, the more it goes on.

Eventually you withdraw. "Sorry, aren't you getting what you want?" I can hear the amusement in your voice. "Do you think it's about your pleasure and you're really in control? Well let's see how you control this?"

This time your cock starts to push at my ass instead. I pull away shaking my head so you push me hard against the wall and carry on. Spreading my cheeks wide with your hands you continue to gently ease yourself into me. I'm wriggling as much as I can to fight you off now. Shaking my head and trying to scream for help pulling wildly at my hands, begging you to stop but the gag takes all the sound from me.

"What's the matter? Are you too good for this kind of fun? Or have you just never done it before?" I'm still shaking my head but you have no idea what I'm shaking my head in response to and don't really care. "Well, I think you'll find I'm in control here so we'll play my way and you'll just have to like it."

Having eased your way all the way inside me you start to fuck me slowly and rhythmically. Holding my hips firm so I don't spoil the sensation for you. I'm still trying to fight you off and I somehow manage to kick you. You yank my head back hard by the hair.

"I really don't think you want to do that again, do you?" Reaching for the knife you return it to my throat and run the blade edge from one side to the other. I've no idea whether you've cut in or not but I can feel the whole length of where it's been. I know you didn't cut hard but that was a lot harder than you'd done it before. Just hard enough to be sufficiently scary for me. Tears start to run down my cheeks as you resume fucking me. Harder this time. It's still not quite right for you though and you look around to see what might help. You withdraw again and remove the gag from my mouth. You grab one wrist, then the other behind me and firmly push me face down over the desk, sliding your cock straight back into me.

There is no gentleness this time, you fuck me hard and relentlessly. Tears are still running from my eyes and I'm squealing through the gag. You decide to be slightly more generous and slide your free hand between my legs to work my clit some more. You realise that I am incredibly turned on by this point and you are so excited by this point that you cum deep and hard inside me.

As soon as you've cum you start to realise what you've done and I realise that you feel bad. You release my hands and untie the gag in my mouth. I turn and look you squarely in the face and then slap you hard once again. This time you just let me.

"Is that it? You're just going to leave me? You've had your fun and that's the end of it? Well I don't think so!" To your complete surprise I lie back on the desk legs spread wide fingers already touching myself.

You obediently drop to your knees and use your tongue and fingers to finally release me. It doesn't take long so you realise how turned on I must have been and I cum loud and hard my whole body convulsing in spasms of pleasure against your fingers and mouth. I climax with an intensity that I haven't felt for years.

I sit up and adjust myself back to some sense of normality.

"Did you really think I'd let you fuck me if I wasn't prepared to go all the way? You were enjoying yourself too much so I thought I'd allow you the feeling of power you evidently wanted. Would it have been as much fun if you hadn't thought you were taking what you wanted against my will? I'll assume that you knew that at least some of my behaviour was acting otherwise you're not a very good boy are you?

Anyway, thanks for the ride but I'm still writing you up………..unless I can come back next week for a repeat inspection and this time we'll do it my way!"

You're standing just looking at me in surprise and all you can think to do is nod. I smile at you, finally adjusting my hair and putting it back up. I grab my clipboard and leave.

Stephen P. Webb - Spring 2018

Tales of the Riverbank Part 1 :

One of the most enjoyable times of my day is when Jess my Labrador Retriever and I head off down the river for our walk. Jess like all her breed is a loving, faithful companion who at times has more resemblance to a soft teddy bear than a descendant of the noble wolf.

She has shared my life for the past thirteen years and I have never seen her have an off day. She's never been anything other than friendly in fact that trait is often her undoing as she can become extremely excitable if she sees a friend and despite three courses at Obedience School I still haven't managed to stop her jumping up to say hello.

This particular habit has lost her a couple of 'friends' in the past but I must say I had a lot of difficulty remaining cross with her as they retreated up the river path complete with muddy paw prints gracing their otherwise pristine clothes.

If Jess has a vice it would be gluttony. Again sharing this trait with her breed Labradors are known as 'walking stomachs' and I've often thought Jess has made it her life's work to test the edibility of whatever comes within snatching distance of her jaws.

Our walk today was in Wellington boots and full waterproof clobber as the rain had steadily fallen for the last three days. The river was swollen and the water was the colour of rich, liquid chocolate. This of course did not deter my water loving hound and she was soon leaping in and swimming with delight wagging her tail like a kind of goofy propeller behind her. The river path was muddy and slippery and I was aware that I couldn't lose myself in too much of a reverie today as I need to be poised for evasive action once Jess decides to pound up the path and shake river water all over me, smiling her little crooked smile.

I loved walking in the rain, you could usually depend on having the river to yourself and that meant an uninterrupted view of the wildlife living along the river banks. Today I was watching the antics of a flock of Yellowhammers. Little birds all squabbling amongst themselves in the branches of a riverside Willow tree. Willows and

Alder trees abound the length of the river and at this time of year are in full leaf, growing together in dense little thickets.

Not taking my own advice about paying close attention I had momentarily lost sight of the dog. This wasn't a particular worry as we both knew every inch of the path and walked it in all weathers, day and night. It was therefore something of a shock to hear

"Gerroff dog" bellowed from the river side of the willow thicket.

With a certain amount of trepidation I ran or more accurately slid, fast and unsteadily over the bank calling for Jess. The sight that met my eyes was a corker. There in the river was a fisherman complete with what looked like an impressive Salmon on his line now also caught in the sleek, ebony jaws of my dog. They seemed to be playing tug-of-war with it.

"Drop that",

I could see the guy was still trying to gain possession of his hard earned prize and had not accepted the unlikelihood of successfully parting a Labrador from an unexpected but altogether welcome snack.

Weighing in to the fray I exhorted my canine to "Leave", and even more authoritatively to "Leave it". Sadly as previously stated the Obedience School was a distant memory for Jess. She'd always lived up to her name and would retrieve any object thrown by any one, any where, however, it would be a warm January before she could ever be convinced to "leave it".

The exasperated fisherman sensing he was in need of reinforcement glared at me and shouted:

"Can't you control your dog? Get it to drop my catch before it's damaged".

Not overly keen on his approach I had to admit the moral high ground was definitely his and so decided I better catch the dog and wrest the blasted fish from her grinning mouth. With no more ado I was down at the water's edge reaching out and grabbing hold of Jess's collar. She was delighted to see me and quite unexpectedly rushed up knocking me down in three feet of water. I however had not let go my grasp on her collar and despite a considerable struggle I felt I was winning. I could feel the wretched fish flapping about, I could certainly smell it. Who in their right mind fishes for pleasure?

The frowning Fisherman had been caught off guard by the reversal in my fortune and was wading over whilst still trying to keep his fishing line taught in the hopes of retrieving his fish. Looking at his facial expression and the tableau we made, it struck me as an extraordinary sight. I could imagine what a third party observer would make of it, it looked for all the world like this guy had caught a fish, a large black dog and a sodden woman and they were all dangling and wriggling about on his line.

Unseemly mirth has often been my down fall in the past, even at school I earned myself a vast number of detentions and had to write reams of lines for laughing and giggling at inappropriate times.

Unfortunately I hadn't learned circumspection, nor had I taken into account the extent of a fisherman's wrath when deprived of his quarry in such a situation. Had I paused for even a moments thought I might have acted differently but …….I laughed.

It wasn't a titter or an amusing snigger it was a full throttle, head thrown back …….. belly laugh. Jess, always one to enjoy a good joke joined in the merriment and promptly plonked herself on top of me driving me under the water.

With a snort of frustration the angry angler threw his rod and keepnet up on to the river bank and with both hands hauled me out from under the dog. She was cavorting around in transports of delight. Great game, lets play again. Panting furiously with her hot pink tongue flapping, she charged about splashing us both and whacking my rescuers legs with her rod like tail. I could hear it slapping against his waders over and over again. Being an experienced dodger of Labrador tails I felt a certain sense of sympathy.

As it turned out I should have saved the sympathy for myself.

Mr humourless the Fishmonger, was not impressed. He dropped me flat on my back on the bank from a great height and failed to hide the smirk of satisfaction my "yeow" elicited. Still standing in the water he leant forward placing his long arms on either side of my head as he brought his face closer and hissed through clenched teeth,

"Do you think this is funny? That was an 8lb Salmon. I was enjoying a peaceful day's fishing before you and your canine fish seeking, exocet missile arrived. I think the least you can do is control yourself if not your dog. I think an apology is in order."

Not moving an inch to allow me to rise I was in a vulnerable position but that didn't stop me from giving him a piece of my mind.

"How dare you! Apologise! Apologise! That's the last thing I'll be doing. You threatened my dog and pushed me under the water to say nothing of slamming me to the ground!"

I wasn't really surprised that he couldn't answer immediately. He'd probably never had to deal with some one who could so misrepresent the actual facts throwing in a bit of dramatic ranting for good measure. Taking advantage of his stunned silence I continued.

"What's a grown man like you doing down here anyway. Torturing wildlife for kicks you should know better. Get yourself a proper hobby."

I couldn't really avoid looking at his face as it was less than a foot from mine. I noted with interest the deep red colour that seemed to suffuse around his cheeks and lips and slowly made its way up towards his forehead.

"Why you little ……."

Almost casually he flipped me over until I was face down in a clump of soaking grass. He grabbed his keep net and brought the wooden handle crashing down on my behind. It made an impressive THWACK as it landed on my riding coat. He repeated this another 5 times. I could feel the force of the strikes but they didn't really make much impression as I was dressed to withstand hurricane force wind and rain and had a number of layers of clothes under my coat.

It was now my turn to try out the stunned silence. I didn't get much of a chance to say anything anyway as he'd pinched my ploy of filling the space with a rant.

My ears were really burning now as he rattled off a list of my offences.

As easily as he'd flipped me over he turned me back and grasping my arms pulled me up until I was at eye level with him. This was only possible as he was still standing below the river bank in the water and I was perched precariously on the muddy bank edge.

"Well. What have you got to say for yourself" He demanded.

I was saved from answering at that moment by my faithful hound. You may have wondered why she hadn't charged to my rescue defending me from such an embarrassing assault on my nether regions.

Truth was Jess had become intrigued by the various bits of fishing kit now haphazardly scattered around us. Always game for a bit of investigation she'd nosed out the fisherman's bag. Feeling that she ought to research the contents of a fishing bag thoroughly for future information she'd managed to flip open the top and low and behold she smelt …..food.

She had distracted our attention with a joyful "Yip" which had us both looking over to where she was excitedly excavating a packet of sandwiches. Suddenly finding ourselves united in wanting to prevent the anticipated sequel to the 'Yip' we both shouted "No" and hurled ourselves at the dog.

In one of those pantomime, slapstick moments we met our fate. On launching myself at Jess I slipped and slid along the muddy bank taking the fisherman down with a low-ish tackle to the thighs knocking him off his feet and by landing on his solar plexus forcing all the air from his lungs.

He then disappeared beneath the water taking me with him. The air which had left in such a hurry was now replaced by muddy river water and seconds later he erupted from the river choking and gagging and generally trying to rip out his trachea. Despite barely breathing and coughing fit to bust a rib he still had a hold of me. I was splashing about trying to regain my footing and generally attempting to prevent even more water soaking into my already sodden clothes when with an enormous heave he forced us both up on to the bank. We landed within inches of my dog who, having enjoyed her unscheduled snack was sitting peaceably on the river bank gently wagging her tail and applauding our performance.

Weak from the exertion and weighed down by about a ton of river water we both sat in bemused silence. He looked over at me and said:

"Are you always this much trouble?"

"What do you mean, it wasn't my fault" I squeaked.

"No? Well I've often wondered. You and your friends have always seemed like trouble at the pub quiz. If you're not arguing with the quizmaster you're trying to cheat with you're answers."
Feeling much maligned I stared at him for a minute. He had a few less layers on now and had lost his silly hat so I could get a reasonable look at the whole of his face. It took a minute but eventually it clicked. He was a friend of my neighbour's who often came to the village at weekends and made up part of the rival team in the bar on quiz night,

"Placed me now have you?" he laughed.

I nodded beginning to feel a tad embarrassed at the situation.

"Look I'm sorry about the sandwiches and the river and things. I live just down here. Do you want to come and dry off and I'll make you some lunch."

"Thank you. If the offer comes with use of a shower I accept . My name's Tony by the way."

It was hardly the time to shake hands and introduce ourselves so I got to my feet and started to pick up some of the detritus now clothing the bank. As we walked and slid our way down the path he put his hand under my arm to steady me. I looked up at him to thank him as he leaned down to me and spoke into my ear.

"I think we need to have a discussion about your behaviour".

He grinned at me and releasing my arm he swatted my bottom with his hand. I didn't know where to look. I especially didn't want him to see the small smile on my face neither did I want to discourage that particular train of thought.

Back at my house I installed Tony in the bathroom shower whilst I popped into the master bedroom ensuite for the fastest shower of my life. I pulled on a comfy pair of tracksuit bottoms with my college sweatshirt and zipping downstairs I hosed the mud off the dog and gave her a brisk rub down with her favourite towel. She plonked down in front of the Aga with a contented sigh sliding gently onto her side preparing to sleep the sleep of the innocent. I nudged her with my foot.

"Hey, you got me spanked on the river bank you know."

Her tail beat a brisk tattoo on the kitchen floor in response to the fondness of my tone. Her gaze focussed on the chopping board where I was cutting sandwiches and making coffee.

"Not a chance" I said, reading her mind and making sure no tidbits were left within reach. I nudged her again whispering:

"Do you think he'll do it again?"

"Oh you can count on that" a deep voice rumbled from the doorway.

He was dressed only in a towel, his hair still damp and curling into little waves around his temple. My eyes scanned his broad shoulders and muscular chest. Evidence of gym membership I thought. He looked fit and his arms, I already knew from being hauled about the river today, were very strong. Perhaps time to reconsider?

With a stage wink he dropped a pile of sopping wet clothes onto the tiled floor and looked longingly over at the sandwiches.

"Oh good FOOD, I'm famished."

Giggling I passed him a plate of ham and cheese sandwiches and poured a steaming mug of coffee for him and whilst his clothes whooshed and whirled in the washing machine we sat at the kitchen table and began those 'getting to know you' conversation strands.

After what seemed like the briefest of interludes he was gathering his gear together and heading off. He paused at the kitchen door to stroke the silky black head attached to the constantly wagging tail.

"See you soon Jess, try and leave the fisherman a few fish," and turning to me with a smile "Will I see you at the Pub Quiz on Friday?"

"A distinct possibility" I laughed.

It was not to be however. Friday was a day of mishap layered on disaster. Work was frenetic and I was too late for the library to return my books and over due DVD rentals. Determined not to extend my fines further, I forced the fat books and DVD cases through the small letter box. When there was no satisfying 'thud' on the other side of the door it became clear that they had became wedged.

I tried a bit of pushing and prodding and when that was unsuccessful gave the area in question a bit of a shove. Well…. whacking great kick actually. This proved to be unwise as a claxon of an alarm peeled out over head. I swear it was loud enough to wake the dead and alert every law enforcement officer in the county including the river police 20 miles away on the Tyne.

Not sure what the protocol should be when caught pounding on the door of a public building I assumed slinking off without trying to at least explain what had happened would be unwise. So pondering on the legal definitions of 'breaking and entering' I didn't have to wait long. A Police patrol car arrived within 10 minutes of the alarm starting followed by another police car some 20 minutes later with a ruffled and far from happy looking Librarian. He had been dragged away from his supper in his role of designated key holder.

The alarm was thankfully deactivated and as my hearing returned to normal I found myself being addressed by two stern Police Officers. One of them was speaking in the lecturing, hectoring kind of tone I remembered from sessions in the Head teacher's office from my schooldays. It was proving to be just as easy to filter it out nodding occasionally to appear compliant and contrite without really processing much of the diatribe.

After a few minutes however the second police officer stepped forward. He lowered his head closer to mine and said:

"Are you always this much trouble?"

My head snapped up and I took a more careful look and sure enough under the regulation uniform cap was the angry angler himself. Oh great. A number of thoughts assaulted my brain simultaneously 'do they still transport prisoners to the colonies?' Probably only those ones they throw the book at and 'surely he wouldn't hold a grudge about that blasted fish ….would he?'

"Tony" I cried and gabbling at 200 words a minute poured out the whole tale. When I ground to a halt he looked over at his colleague who shrugged his shoulders. I could see he was trying not to smile.

"It's a pretty extreme way of avoiding a fine on your library books" he said a slow grin turning up the corners of his mouth.

Thankfully they seemed to think it was more amusing than criminal and following a sincere apology to the Librarian for trouble caused, the evidence of my breaking and entering career was put to one side.

Tony drew me aside and quietly spoke into my ear.

"Well we'll not be short of discussion topics when we meet up" He said.

I felt a certain tingling in my stomach as I said "will you be at the Quiz night to night?"

"Sadly not my shift's altered. I'll catch up with you though. You know what they say about the long arm of the law!"

Saturday dawned with wonderful streaks of amber and crimson staining the sky. As I stood at my bedroom window overlooking the river I could see acres of sky painted ever colour of blue from duck egg to navy where clouds still held a little rain. It wasn't raining today though so I determined on an early stroll along the river path to blow away the cobwebs and my brush with the law.

Jess, always happy to accompany me on my walks, commenced her "we are going walking" Cha Cha Cha. She could keep it up for quite a while whilst I found walking boots, coat, hat and lead. She accompanied the Cha Cha with a little whiney song which was delivered in little rising trills becoming higher in pitch and incredibly shrill by the time your hand was on the door latch.

Released from the confines of the house she belted along the river path stopping briefly to woof at the little Mallard chain gang who rushed up expectantly for breakfast.

My neighbour usually distributed a few handfuls of duck feed before work but as it was the weekend he was obviously having a lie in. One petite, dowdy brown female had settled herself on my front doorstep and unbothered by the canine bulldozer as she charged past, was calmly preening her downy breast feathers. I wondered if she'd still be there on our return and made a mental note to stop off at the Village Shop for bread.

The river path quickly leaves the village behind weaving into the 'Enchanted Glade' - my description of a shaded area overhung with Hawthorn and Holly trees. Swathed beneath the tree trunks later in the year would be a carpet of wood anemones with white petals which shimmer in contrast to the deep emerald green of their leaves and stems. Today though, as I pushed through the green boughs leading to the kissing gate my senses absorbed wave after wave of the piquant aroma of wild garlic.

Jess has used her dog's entrance – a large whole in the fence and as I opened the gate the vista of the river was revealed before me snaking up the river valley in all its majesty. The water is clear, almost translucent today and we pause to choose some interesting pebbles. They gleam like jewels until you take them from their setting and as they dry out they become dull and flat in the light.

Jess selects her usual boulders far too large to be put in my pocket so I employ a bit of magicians sleight of hand to replace them with ones of more suitable weight. She drops a large one on my toe and as I call her on I throw it far out across the river and laugh as she dives into the water to give chase.

We take the upper path today and she races ahead tale wagging in circles as she runs. The path skirts the edge of a cultivated field on the right hand side and from our elevated height we can look down into the river cutting ever more deeply through the earth as it winds into a wide arc.

The field had barley and oilseed rape harvested earlier in the year leaving behind sharp hard stalk stubble which scratches unprotected legs. It doesn't seem to bother Jess and I wait with a sense of anticipation for her next game to begin.

Before she makes it half way across the field several Ringed Plovers take to the air. These ground nesting birds have intriguing ways of protecting their young. In order to distract potential predators one of the parent birds feigns injury and limps, hops and flies around drawing the predator away from their nests. This is far too subtle for Jess so they swoop down and fly extremely low just ahead of her. This is a hugely favourite game and she rushes about following wherever they lead.

As I walk on the path starts to decline and I am once again at the river's edge. The Plovers are still playing with Jess when a large dappled brown hare lollops across my path. He was close enough to touch and I watched as he sat down to scratch his long ears. Moments later he was running smoothly in a straight line towards my dog attracted by her weaving about. So much for predator and prey!

This adult hare was in no danger from Jess she'd never caught or killed anything her whole life but she did enjoy to chase. So did the hare as it turned out. He joined the game twisting and turning teasing my poor dog who never got close. I was by this time laughing inelegantly and with considerable volume when I heard

"You're scaring the fish."

Scanning the riverbank I made out a bipedal shape pushing through a stand of willow withies. PC Angry Angler was on duty only today he didn't look angry, far from it. He joined me on the path and we stood together watching the Labrador's ineffectual attempts to round up half a dozen Plovers and a Hare. He had to admit it was a comical sight and soon his laughter mingled with mine.

Jess on becoming a little puffed searched around for me. On

spotting not only me but a 'friend' she came at full pelt. Tony was unprepared for the onslaught and stood unsuspecting as I with my superior knowledge and yen for survival, manoeuvred myself onto a flatter stretch of the path ready to perform the Matador leap of which I am an expert proponent.

I still maintain to this day that I warned Tony in ample time for him to take evasive action. He on the other hand declares I set him up by moving so that he would turn to keep me in view thus leaving his back unprotected and a substantial target.

Jess had achieved a record speed by the time she came barrelling over the edge of the field. My cry of "watch out" quickly followed by "DOWN" had him swivelling about hands flapping as though under attack by a swarm of bees.

Too little too late, 25kgs of dog landed full square against his upper thighs. Her velocity carried him through the air and man and dog executed a neat parabola before crashing to the floor and rolling a ways through the prickly stemmed wild rhubarb leaves.

The contents of Tony's bag were cast with an expert fly fishing technique reaching a considerable distance across the river. Various objects could be seen floating away in the meandering current one of which looked suspiciously like a packet of sandwiches.

Looking down at my dog I could see she was conflicted…..stay and play licking the face of the nice man or retrieve…..play or retrieve….. After a few cursory licks to the accompaniment of some extraordinary language from Tony, she followed her strongest urge and sailed over the river bank into the river.

I could positively feel the millions of olfactory cells in her nose kick into gear as in very few seconds she honed in on the sandwich bag which had sailed quite a few yards further down river. She altered course and swam off in pursuit of another unscheduled snack in high satisfaction.

This of course left me with an extremely exasperated, although still winded, fisherman once again deprived of his peaceful hobby, to say nothing of his sandwiches, and items of fisherman mystery now sailing down the Coquet to the sea.

It's possible I could have averted disaster, calming the situation with apologies and offers of replacement foodstuffs. However this was a moot point as alas, my reaction, swiftly following the 'rooted to the ground', frozen, shocked, horrified concerned citizen bit, was to throw myself to the ground clutching my stomach as I howled with unrelenting laughter.

I couldn't see Tony's expression as he disentangled himself from the Velcro like stems of the rhubarb fronds. Nor as he collected his now empty bag and gazed about in an aimless attempt to recover vital angling equipment. What I did see was the look on his face when he loomed over me shaking his head in disbelief. I think he was trying to speak but only spluttering blustery sounds were pouring forth fuelled by my uncontrollable mirth. I was in pain. My sides were aching and I wasn't able to take enough breath to speak let alone drag myself to my feet.

I didn't have to try that as I felt strong hands on my arms firmly lifting me up. I didn't however stay up very long as I found myself hoisted under Tony's arm and perched on his hip. He marched a few feet to the base of an ancient oak tree and sat himself on the raised root bed placing me face down over his lap.

Still hiccoughing with laughter I couldn't do anything to resist and it wasn't until I felt my coat wrenched up above my waist and my track suit bottoms sliding down below my hips that I began to comprehend my vulnerability. Wriggling with a will at this point I managed to slide down his waders but wasn't successful in getting a purchase with my feet to stand up before I was caught around the waist in an iron grip and held securely against his body.

"I am most definitely going to enjoy this you hooligan."

And with that he rained a volley of sharp spanks down on my unprotected behind. SMACK………SMACK …..SMACK. He delivered a trio of crisp slaps to my left buttock and then three more to my right. He paused between each slap giving them time to sink in. I could certainly feel the full force of these and wished for a couple of layers of jumpers to deaden the sting like before.

Not having ever been spanked I'd no experience with which to compare. The spanks he'd given me so far were firm and there was a sting after each one landed but it didn't really hurt.

Tony delivered another round of spanks moving around my buttocks and aiming a few firm smacks to the upper thighs. I didn't like that and my Ouch's went up in pitch and volume.

"That's ok for your warm up" he said "Now lets see if you find this funny"

He began to spank at a rhythmical pace, giving time between each spank but moving his hand around to cover all over my bottom.

"Tony" I wailed trying to free myself. He gently placed his hand on the small of my back saying

"Ssshh.. you're going to enjoy this".

With that he picked up the tempo alternating between gentle slaps and harder spanks keeping me guessing. He was still being fairly light handed but definitely making an impression as my gasps and yelps confirmed. He stopped spanking and rubbed the flesh, kneading his fingers into my buttocks drawing breathy sighs from me.

Slowly he pushed down my panties revealing nicely pink and slightly quivering buttocks. He gently caressed the area where thighs and buttocks meet and without warning he spanked down hard. There was a crack like the report of a gun. I squealed and gasped holding my breath in anticipation of the next one.

"Young lady, I believe you owe me an apology"

SLAP. Another whack, the force of which shifted me along his lap. I gasped again biting my lip waiting with all my concentration for the next one.

"You and your unbelievably disobedient dog have spoiled yet another days fishing for me and you do not appear to be treating this with the gravity it deserves"

SLAP…. SMACK…….SLAP…….SMACK…….SLAP……..SMACK

A volley of lighter spanks this time had me writhing against his legs.

Too many sensations followed too closely together for me to process what I was feeling but I knew I wanted him to stop about as much as I wanted him to continue.

"I'll take that apology now little one" SPANK…. SPANK… SPANK another trio to the right and then the left cheek.

"I'm sorry" I groaned.

"Are you going to interfere with my fishing again?"

"NO"!

"Are you going to resume obedience classes for you and that sandwich stealing mutt?"

"Yes, yes I promise"

"Good. Are you going to invite me home so that we can finish off this discussion?"

As I answered "OK" I was aware that my voice was husky and deep in pitch and my mouth was so dry I didn't attempt to say anything further.

Tony replaced my track suit trousers and hoisted me to my feet planting a firm full lipped kiss on my mouth. Taking my hand he showed just how well he'd come to know at least one of the females in the anti fishing league as he yelled

"Jess dinner time" and as if by magic my dripping smiling friend appeared and ran after us down the river path home.

Tales of the River bank Part 2

Jess and the Sheep

Standing on the ancient stone bridge in front of my house and looking down river, I tried to gauge whether the river level had subsided sufficiently to take my faithful black Labrador Jess on her favourite walk. For several days the river had been in spate following heavy rain and seasonal high tides and had flooded the river path making it inaccessible from the village. It looked as though it had receded significantly and so I determined to give it a go. Jess would be in her element no matter what as she loved any excuse to get wet and in the height of summer had been known to sit in tiny rain puddles to refresh herself, if deprived of the river or beach.

Being less excited by muddy river water than my dog I prepared for waterlogged ground and put on my tallest Wellington boots and took my walking crook for leverage to deal with any clinging, sticky mud.

Before setting off I sat Jess down in the kitchen and prepared to deliver some sage advice. She adopted her 'I'm not really focussed on my dog lead' look and attempted to concentrate on my oratory.

"Now listen, its going to be very wet down the river today and likely very muddy as well. Your paws will be wet and muddy too, so………. NO JUMPING UP …got it?"

Jess with tongue wagging and smiling face gave me total body language confirmation of her comprehension of my order and I felt a certain confidence that we would have no mishaps today. Unfortunately for me there were one or two of our acquaintances who seemed always to blame me for my dog's misbehaviour and I was not wanting to face any consequences for canine unruliness today.

Binoculars in hand, canine perfectly to heel we exited the house and joined the river path. The water was tripping along over the clumps of sandstone slabs which formed the bedrock of the river bottom, swirling here and there in little whirlpools and washing up against the bank to caress and bathe the over hanging branches of the water loving trees.

Scanning ahead my attention was immediately directed to two salmon carcasses caught in clumps of alder. This sometimes happened when, during the salmon spawning runs, older specimens were overwhelmed by the sheer force of the river and their bodies were deposited on the river bank or left in higher branches of the willow and alder bushes as the river levels fell.

These fish, some of prodigious size, where left as food for opportunist hunters and scavengers alike. I was alerted to their presence by the congregation of crows and jackdaws that were dining in their usual raucous fashion. Ripping flesh from the remains and hopping about with it trying to retain possession whilst being pursued by hungry hangers on. I warned Jess to stay at heel and was pleased to her comply for once as we passed the danger zone.

At this time of year I needed to be watchful for such carrion as my companion waged a constant war with the sin of gluttony. As with many of her breed she was obsessed with food. I had many times watched her dilemma, when confronted with a stinking, rotting carcass, particularly a dead fish. She would appear conflicted about whether to roll in the remains, thus adorning her beautiful shiny coat with putrid, rancid, greeny grey, gloopy flesh, the smell of which could halt traffic, or to eat it. If allowed sufficient time with such a windfall her response of course would be to do both.

On this particular walk I was determined to be vigilant and to prevent such gastronomic indiscretion. So hurrying along I kept Jess focussed on chasing and retrieving her toys and having a swim in a corpse free section of the river. Suspecting I would be wise to take the upper path today away from the water's edge we strode off up the farm track towards the fields.

There were swathes of delicate wild flowers clothing the field boundaries and path today, sweet white and yellow field pansies nodding above bright blue speedwell growing in little cushions close to the ground, long spikes of purple vetch with its delicate tendrils twinning around taller grass stalks leading the eye to a swathe of Lady's Mantle with its soft green leaves and heads of tiny yellow green flowers. Many of these plants with their evocative names grow in quiet profusion on these less travelled paths. As the year progresses they will give way to groves of pink and white Foxgloves and drifts of the elegant Rose Bay Willow Herb.

We could hear grasshoppers scratching out their chorus interspersed by the 'chock chock' of strutting pheasants all in relief against the gurgling and murmuring backdrop of the busy river as it sped down through the valley. Lulled into a vacant musing I was at peace with the world and enjoying my solitary ramble. Jess was off scooting through the oil seed rape stalks and had gone so far over she could no longer locate me. I laughed as every so often she would appear above the drying crop, leaping up to catch a view of me, her ears rising up above her head as though they were applauding.

It was whilst hovering above the crop that she spotted one of her friends galloping up to meet her. Shooting past me like a rocket, Romulus the wire haired grey lurcher sped in a direct line towards Jess. There were sounds of canine greetings followed by a frantic game of chase. The two dogs bowled out of the field and thundered away up the path. Romulus was faster but Jess more solid and not above giving her slim friend a violent body check in order to gain the lead. Depending on whether he had managed a defensive stance Romulus would either be knocked violently off course or if Jess's aim was true he could be floored and watching his competitors heels disappearing into the distance.

Pausing at the height of the paths' incline I waited for Romulus's master Geoff to catch up. He, like me, was making slower progress due to several pounds of mud adhering to the soles of his boots. We chatted as we walked along watching our dogs in their delighted gambolling. He talked of his work on his latest commission. As a wildlife sound recordist he travelled all over the country and abroad tracking down rare or unrecorded animal and bird sounds. His work was in demand and he had several projects on the go.

We laughed about the recent Barn Owl recording fiasco and he took the opportunity to remind me that he had been an auditory witness to a spanking I had received from a fisherman friend. I still found it very embarrassing that he knew about Tony and I and was very happy when he reassured me that his lips were sealed and it would go no further.

Heading on the downward slope which would reunite us with the river just before it carved a long slow bend, we paused as a brown streak shot across the path into the undergrowth ahead of us. Moments later frantic squeaking was heard and the stoat appeared his jaws gripping a limp vole. That was more of a glimpse of this dedicated hunter than was usual, normally a brown blur was all you would see.

The river bend came into view a stunning panorama on this still day. The enormous panoply of sky, a bright, bright blue providing a perfect back drop for the patchwork of fields dressed in their vast array of greens, browns and dun colour, highlighted at intervals by the stunning yellow of gorse flowers. I never tired of this view and as we stood admiring the vista with the exotic coconut fragrance of the gorse wafting up to excite our senses further, we noted …………..the absence of dogs.

Normally the dogs would have circled back to us by now keen to share their joyful enthusiasm before rushing off again to continue the adventure. We scanned ahead searching for signs of activity near the water's edge whilst Geoff whistled a shrill recall command for Romulus. Nothing. This did not bode well. Exchanging suspicions regarding rotting fish we trotted down the hill each calling for our hounds.

Nearing the bottom of the slope we were nearly knocked off our feet as the two miscreants exploded up the steep river bank dragging what looked like an enormous woolly blanket filled with sticks all jutting out at sharp angles. Closer inspection of their treasure as it flew past us identified it as the remains of a sheep carcass. Somewhat stunned at the speedy turn of events we could only watch as the dogs tore off back up the hill giving the impression of two galloping horses trailing a war chariot behind them.

Galvanised into activity worthy of the Key Stone Cops in their hay day, Geoff and I gave chase. Arms flailing, shouting orders, we attempted to shift up a gear trying vainly to force our feet faster from the ground to which they were glued by viscous mud. We gave only a poor 'B movie' impression of foot soldiers following the chariots into battle, the chariot in question, having sailed over the hill top, and out of sight.

Before long the sound of the dogs returning had us jumping to the side of the path to avoid the onslaught. The sight that met our eyes had us roaring with laughter. Somehow in their crazy tug of war over the carcass, it had been flipped up and was now resting along Romulus' back. Jess not prepared to lose such an unexpected and delicious snack was still hanging on to it running in Romulus' wake looking like a bridesmaid holding the brides train.

The dogs cut down in front of me heading back to the river. Purely out of reflex I dived forward and grabbed the carcass which slid off the lurcher's back. Deprived of his mutton cloak he flipped around and snatched a mouthful grabbing part of the remains of a leg and some fleece. Both dogs were firmly tugging at the carcass heading down the riverbank but now trailing me on my stomach clutching at the bag of bones for dear life.

Gripping firmly to the fleece and yelling at the dogs to 'leave it' I was dragged inexorably towards the edge of the riverbank. My nose was in extremely close proximity to what was, I now realised, a very old, very smelly and waterlogged sheep's carcass. It had probably washed down river during the flooding and had been caught up in debris in the water for some time.

Unpleasant as it was to be grasping such remains I was relentless, determined not to concede it to the dogs knowing they would be very sick if they managed to eat any of it. As the dogs pulled me over the steep bank dredging me through the thick grasping mud and various flotsam deposited by the ebbing waters, Geoff, incapacitated by gales of laughter finally caught us up. His breathing was still too ragged for much of an attempt at canine control but he managed to gasp out "let go" to me.

Trying a more determined shout he yelled

"Let go, they're going to pull you in the river."

Sticking like a burr, I held on just about processing what Geoff was shouting as he became more frantic. When it became obvious I wasn't about to relinquish my hold Geoff threw himself down on the riverbank edge and grabbed my legs as they slithered over.

Much later it occurred to me what a ridiculous sight this would have made. We now had a canine versus human tug of war with a decaying sheep's carcass and a short human female stretched out as the rope. As neither side showed signs of relenting so battle was joined. Geoff's grunts of effort were punctuated by staccato demands that I

"Let go…… for god's sake let go"

The dogs thoroughly enjoying the day's sport were growling continuously their voices harmonising as they worried the flesh trapped in their jaws.

Still gripping tight to promote my claim on the carcass I could feel Geoff losing purchase on my legs. He'd grabbed hold of my wellies at calf level and whilst he hung on with a vice like grip the wellies were gradually being dragged off my legs.

Disaster was imminent the dogs had reached the water and I was being dragged closer to the pebbly beach heading towards the mocha coloured water. Fearing the worst Geoff launched a last ditch attempt to get me to release my hold. Shimmying forward to pin my feet under his chest he took aim and crashed his open palm down on my backside.

"Yeow …… hey" I shouted.

"Let go you idiot" he retorted and putting all his weight into it he whacked his hand again and again down on my perfectly positioned bottom. It felt like an anvil falling repeatedly on my vulnerable nether region and after several resounding wallops I released the carcass.

Geoff hauled me back up the bank plonking me aside on a grassy mound. Having regained my senses I retaliated for what I considered had been an unprovoked attack by punching Geoff's arm and delivering a shower of rhetoric expressing my ire at his high handed treatment. We were exchanging blows and generally tumbling about when, exasperated, and concerned for his personal safety, Geoff pushed me off him rolling me over and pinning me face down over the grassy mound. He wrestled my coat up and exposed my bottom. He then proceeded to make it extremely clear that he wasn't impressed with my response to his gallant rescue of me by walloping me with sharp stinging spanks. There was no pause between them they rained down like rapid gunfire, pop, pop, pop, pop, pop, pop, pop.

All attempts to free myself from his grasp failed so in desperation I yelled for Jess to help me. This caused a great guffaw of laughter from Geoff who rolling me back over indicated I should look to my left. Sitting up I could see both dogs lying together in a heap tongues lolling, smiling broad contented grins as they watched my paddling with great good humour.

So much for having a dog for protection I thought. Beckoning Jess over to me I fondled her ears as I checked for any bits of carcass that may have got lodged in her collar.

"You've done it again dog" I murmured to her "Got me spanked by the river"

Looking up into my face her tail wagging madly I could almost have sworn that she winked.

Stephen P. Webb - Spring 2018

For the Sake of Her Art :

Maggie Breen was excited. Inspiration had come to her in the night and she now knew for certain what she would create for her exhibition piece. In her final year of a Fine Arts degree, Maggie was due to produce a centre piece for an exhibition of her classmates work at the prestigious Laing Gallery. Her work was to reflect her interest in creative photography and up until 2 hours ago, she had yet to decide her theme.

Mulling over all the elements she'd wanted to include in her piece her subconscious had finally woven the threads into an idea and now she felt ready to make a start on the design for it. She had settled on a giant montage with many tiny photographs united on a canvas to create a larger picture, broadly in the fashion of the cubists who created their wonderfully vibrant paintings from thousands of tiny dots of colour.

Maggie was fascinated by movement and had always striven to capture the energy of speed and power on film. Her work had a reputation for its originality and never failed to incite comment and usually a degree of excitement. A recent series of photographs that she had taken from her friend's car window as they travelled at night up the motorway, at high speed, had created a stunning mix of colour from the head and tail lights of passing cars as they swirled and leapt in shapes and slashes across her film. She'd received praise from her Professors and plaudits from a number of organisations who had used or displayed her work. Unfortunately, for Maggie all this did was to increase expectations for the final crowning exhibition.

Given that she now knew what she wanted to do as her subject matter, Maggie considered her strategy planning, and how best to achieve the shots she needed. During her time at University, Maggie had photographed a vast array of student activities. She'd focussed on fast paced sports, in order to refine her techniques to capture dynamic motion. In particular, she enjoyed photographing rowing which seemed to embrace all of the elements she was looking for in her work.

The University had a thriving rowing club who were currently engaged in rigorous training in the lead up to the regatta season.

Maggie spent time photographing them as they trained every morning, capturing them, as the boats ploughed their way up river, striving for perfection and battling the elements.

Maggie's shots focussed on the boat and its relationship with the water, as well as the energy and power of the rowers as they strived to achieve a consistent momentum. She contemplated how she could persuade them to allow her access to their inner sanctum, to shoot the additional reams of film of their preparation, training and rowing needed for her project.

Up until now, Maggie had preferred to observe life around her and largely record its rhythms on film. She had taken little active part in student life. She had few close friends on campus and none at all on the rowing team. She was aware that the rowing club was held in very high regard by the University and that the current teams boasted a record of winning more successive races than ever before in the history of the club. The rowers were totally dedicated to their sport and as a consequence of the demands of their training programme, were infrequently seen at student social events. This increased the perception of them as an elite, rather insular group which made Maggie's task of gaining their cooperation with the next stages of her project more difficult.

Working in the College photographic suite later that morning Maggie shared her dilemma with Gemma, one of her classmates. Gemma was the antithesis of Maggie. She knew everyone on campus by sight, had been to every social event going in her three years at University and judging by the stories she related, she had dated virtually every male within the college aegis. It therefore came as no surprise to learn that she had dated members of the rowing club.

She listened as Maggie outlined what she needed, and after a couple of moments thought, she suggested introducing Maggie to her one of her ex-boyfriends, Paul. She explained that the rowing club had a hierarchical structure with a President and officials elected from the members at the beginning of each season. In order to be allowed access to training sessions Maggie would need the consent of the President and the governing committee. It was her view that such a request would meet with more favour if it was sponsored by a member of the club, and that this was where Joel would come in.

Before Maggie could even properly process what Gemma had said, Gemma had things arranged. Maggie would meet Joel in the Student Union Bar that evening and outline her project to him.

As a consequence, 7pm found Maggie nursing a glass of dry white wine in the bar waiting a little anxiously for Joel to arrive. She wasn't used to discussing her work with non- artists and wasn't convinced of her ability to convey her ideas successfully. She was fidgeting on her bar stool absentmindedly shredding a tissue with her fingers when a deep voice behind her said

"It surrenders"

She looked around puzzled and came face to muscular chest with Joel. When her eyes had risen to seek his face she could see he was indicating the tissue with a grin.

"Hi" she said shyly "Thanks for coming. What will you have?"

Paul indicated the bitter and she collected a pint for him before moving to join him at a table away from the crush at the bar. Succumbing to nerves Maggie sat silently staring into her drink. She was fighting an internal battle with herself, trying to force herself to take charge of the situation and explain what she needed to Joel. Amused by her obvious discomfort, Joel waited giving her time to settle herself and begin.

After quite a long pregnant pause Paul relented, and helped Maggie out, by asking some preliminary questions about her course and her photographic interests. Finding her way with these familiar topics Maggie began to relax and soon was speaking with enthusiasm and revealing her passion for her creative process. Joel considered her, enchanting. He could discern her drive and creative urge from the way she spoke of her work and she seemed unaware of the fire that lit in her eyes as she did so, totally transforming her usually guarded expression with joyful overtones. His interest piqued, Joel gently drew the details of her project from Maggie. He confirmed what she felt she wanted, with what would be possible without interfering with the training regime of the rowers, and he said that he didn't think they would have any problem with supporting Maggie in approaching the President of the club.

He suggested she meet him at lunch time the next day at the clubhouse when he would be able to introduce her to Jim Taylor the President. She agreed happily and headed back to her flat with ideas and images buzzing around her head.

The next day, Maggie joined Joel at the clubhouse at noon. Maggie was almost hyperventilating, as her project was all she could think about. The urge to begin taking the photos and building her montage was so strong it was almost tangible. Sensing her heightened emotions and ragged breathing, Paul took her hand almost as if without that link tethering her to earth, she might float away. Her hand trembled in his as he gave it a reassuring squeeze. Following Paul's introduction, and with his help, Maggie presented her request and discussed her ideas for the montage. Jim listened carefully, finally nodding and smiling at her.

"It sounds like quite an ambitious project Maggie. I don't really foresee any difficulties with you photographing the teams and covering training and prep sessions but I will have to formally propose your request to the committee"

"I see" said Maggie looking a little dejected.

"Don't worry we're meeting today so I'll be able to give you a decision later on. Can you come back about 3 o'clock?"

"Oh yes, great, ……..thank you" she gushed.

Hardly able to wait until 3 o'clock Maggie tried to concentrate on her preliminary outline for the montage. She liked to work with filters, to capture the subtle nuances of colour within shade and she prepared her bag with a range of filters and different speed film in order to experiment with shots of the river.

At the appointed time, she knocked on the clubhouse door and was admitted in by Jim. He introduced her to his Vice President, Quentin Cousins, the Treasurer, Tom Robertson and Adam Farley who he laughingly introduced as 'member without specific portfolio' and Joel who it turned out, was also the Junior Coach for the first eight.

Jim guided her to a seat at their table. She felt like she was in an interview and began to feel a prickly sensation at her neck. Jim smiled at her and explained that they were all in agreement, and that she would be granted access for her 'fly on the wall' shots.

There were however some stipulations. The Club's primary purpose was to produce
successful rowing teams to compete at the highest levels of collegiate competition. Nothing would be allowed to interfere with this goal or to tarnish the reputation of the Club. He further explained that because they were in competition with other Colleges and Clubs that it was important that Maggie respect their confidentiality particularly, regarding training techniques and schedules. She would have to agree not to disclose any information concerning the Club to any third party and to sign a declaration confirming this commitment. Should she fail to respect this important condition she would also have to accept the ensuing "consequences".

Maggie happily agreed to these conditions and signed the declaration document, knowing she would do nothing to jeopardize her project and as her worst fear was that she would be forbidden access to the Club, she could think of no worse consequence of reneging on their agreement.

It was agreed between them, that Joel would act as a guide and liaison for Maggie. He gave her the training and practice schedules for the next two weeks and exchanged mobile phone numbers with her. She would begin by photographing the first eight on their warm up runs on the river in the morning.

Over the next few days, everything proceeded well. Maggie haunted the rowing club, becoming a recognised addition prowling around at the edge of action, shrewdly recording with her mind's eye and capturing moments of vibrant activity, transforming these fleeting samples of human endeavour into a lasting visual testimony. She was so engrossed that she was unaware of the interest she aroused, and this in itself ensured that the rowers quickly became accustomed to her presence and behaved naturally around her.

Rushing to the photographic suite with rolls of film for processing, Maggie felt alive and enriched. She loved the pictures she was achieving. Everything she had hoped about this subject was emerging in the proofs and she began to transfer small images to her larger montage.

Utterly focussed on her art other aspects of Maggie's life evaded her. She wasn't sleeping very much preferring to work on whenever she felt her muse was strongest. She wasn't eating very much either as she sublimated bodily needs to what she felt was her creative imperative.

The fact that she was fading away was not lost on the people around her. Gemma had taken to leaving packets of sandwiches in the darkroom hoping that Maggie would eat reflexively if she happened on them. Paul had on occasion bodily removed her from the rowing gym and sat her in front of a plate of vegetable lasagne from the canteen. He had not been amused when on returning to see if she wanted dessert, he found her photographing his team mates in the act of conveying vast quantities of food to their mouths, her own barely touched and congealing, abandoned, on her plate.

Towards the end of the first fortnight Gemma succeeded in extricating Maggie from the darkroom to join her at a concert on campus. They went with a group of Gemma's friends and were soon fully engaged, letting their hair down, dancing and singing along with the band. In the bar afterwards the fun continued. Maggie enjoying the down time, allowed herself to be carried along with the group as they went to a night club. Drinks were flowing and Maggie far exceeded her usual limited intake. This combined with a general lack of sustenance over the last two weeks led to a very swift reaction. She began to feel a little woozy and sat down, slightly groggily, at Gemma's friend's table.

She found her usual inhibitions with strangers were relaxed. She was talking incessantly and judging by their responses she was a hit, very humorous and witty. Responding to questions from some of the group she began to relay anecdotes from her recent observations at the rowing club. These clearly met with approval because she found herself questioned more closely about what she was photographing there, how often she went and the range of activities she observed. With no sense that what she was doing was wrong, she continued to chat and answer these questions until she found herself propelled towards the exit, a large hand with strong fingers on her arm and another around her shoulders.

Emerging into the cool night air Maggie felt her head swim and her vertical hold release. She would have landed on the hard pavement had not the large hands caught her. Attempting to focus on the owner of the hands she registered some of what was being muttered, none to gently in her ear. It was Paul and he was now hoisting her up in his arms and stomping off across the quad towards the housing block. His muttering persisted and she caught odd phrases such as 'little idiot', 'plastered' 'no sense' 'spilling everything to the competition', but she wasn't really in shape to comprehend their import. Lying back in Paul's arms she began to hum a jaunty little refrain which served only to inspire louder mutterings interspersed with the occasional oath.

With no understanding or memory of how she got there Maggie awoke the next morning with a raging thirst and a punishing headache. When she managed to open her eyes fully she noted she was in her own room, fully clothed in last nights' jeans and v necked top, wrapped in her duvet. Sitting up she attempted to walk to the bathroom but found her legs uncooperative. She sank back into her bed and closed her eyes once more.

Becoming aware of a regular beat resounding in her head, consciousness returned. She lay for a while considering if the knocking sound was coming from her brains as they reverberated inside her skull. She eventually decided it wasn't her brains, the knocking was external. Opening her eyes she focussed on the digital clock on the night stand. It read 3.40. Now that surely couldn't be AM could it? Scanning the room she decided it was light out and so must be 3.40pm. 3.40PM……… she'd slept right through the day!

Scrabbling to get out of bed she localised the banging sound. It was someone at her door. Wrapped in her duvet she stepped towards the door placing her feet gingerly so as not to jar the unrestrained cerebral matter which was pounding the inside of her head. Grasping the door handle she peered around the door and came face to face with a large glass of fresh orange juice. Grabbing it with both hands she retreated into her room sipping thirstily and moaning with pleasure as the cold liquid revived her parched throat.

She felt herself guided to a chair and a take out container with toast and scrambled eggs was placed in front of her. Groaning as her stomach flipped over she pushed the box away and focussed on the extremely large person who was leaning over her. Paul.

She tried a nonchalant "Hi" but it sounded like a rusty hinge squeaking and so she gave up on oral communication in favour of hydration and continued to sip her juice. Kneeling at her side Paul held out a slice of toast indicating she should eat it. Shaking her head she felt him take her hand and enclose it around the toast.

"Eat it" he ordered and headed to the galley kitchen where he proceeded to crash the kettle about and generally make a symphony of noise. He even managed a jet of water from the tap which sounded like a fire hose on full pressure. He returned with some aspirin and a large mug of black coffee. Again pushing the toast to her lips he said,

"You better get in the shower. An extraordinary committee meeting has been called for 5pm at the club and you need to attend it."

Shaking her head Maggie tried to recover cerebral function and to scan recent memory to see if she knew about this meeting. Nothing came to mind but as she was being encouraged into the bathroom by a large, and she was beginning to suspect less than happy, rower she decided a shower was a good plan. The waterfall which emerged from the usually dribbling shower head succeeded in completing whatever brain damage had been caused by the earlier banging and as she tentatively rubbed her hair dry, aiming for the least possible movement of her head, she wondered what this meeting was about?

Scouring the bedroom for some fresh clothes she tried some of the coffee and felt a little better. Resumption of some of her faculties had her observing Paul as he sat waiting for her. Definitely not happy she decided. In fact he looked to be in a reverie vibrating with suppressed emotion.

Sensing her presence Joel leapt to his feet and taking her arm propelled Maggie through the door saying:

"Come on you don't need to be late on top of everything else"

They made it to the club house minutes before 5 o'clock with Maggie still peppering Paul with questions. All he had said in answer to her queries was

"Think carefully about what happened last night".

Not being able to relate any of the events of the previous night to the rowing club Maggie remained confused. On entering the Clubhouse, Maggie could see the four members of the committee sitting on chairs in a semi circle. Paul ushered her forward until she was standing in front of them. He continued to stand with her but took a pace behind her.

As she scanned the faces seated before her Maggie felt her mouth dry and she began to feel uncomfortable. Jim spoke first,

"Maggie we've asked you to come before the committee to discuss a report which reached us." He paused watching her carefully and could see a look of confusion on her face, but not as yet, any dawning of comprehension as to the reason for her predicament.

"We have learned that last evening you regaled a number of rowers from a rival club with specific details and information concerning our training and preparations for competition."

Maggie gasped shaking her head in denial and staring at Jim in incomprehension.

"Do you deny the charge Maggie?" He asked.

"Yes, yes I do. I haven't talked to any rowers from anywhere," she retorted.

"Where you at Dante's Night Club last evening?" he continued

"Yes" she replied "With my friend Gemma and some of her mates".

Jim watched as it became clear that the penny had dropped. He watched realisation course across Maggie's face as a blush sneaked up her cheeks.

"Oh no" she breathed. "They were…… rowers?"

Jim nodded. "Do you remember what you told them?" he asked

"Not everything" She replied in a small voice. "We weren't there that long." she whined.

"You were not there long only because Paul removed you from the nightclub, is how I understand it. ……… Isn't that correct?"

Maggie turned to look at Paul and nodded.

"If Paul hadn't happened to be there and to have overheard you, the situation could have been much more serious for our club" lectured Jim.

Maggie was consumed with guilt. If truth be told she only had the vaguest memory of what she'd said at the nightclub last night, but she did remember anecdotes about certain rowers coming up.

Fearing what Jim would say next she slowly regained eye contact with him.

"We hold you to have broken our agreement and as such are no longer disposed to grant you access to the club"

Maggie's heart turned over as she cried out:

"Oh please, not that. I'm really sorry. I was stupid and a little drunk. I didn't intend to break the agreement. I'm really sorry. I hope no damage has been done. Please don't ban me I still need more photographs. Please." She pleaded with them, desperation written large upon her face.

Jim looked over to Quentin who spoke:

"Paul has pleaded your case to us Maggie. We accept that there was no deliberate intent on your part to damage the club. However when you accepted the terms of our agreement you acknowledged that breach of the conditions would lead to consequences. We understand how serious it would be for your project if you could not continue to take your photographs and so, at Paul's urging, we are minded to consider an alternative to banning you."

Unbelievably relieved, Maggie quickly said,

"Oh thank you, thank you very much. I really am very sorry, I'd like to make amends if I can."

Quentin held up his hand to halt Maggie's flow of speech.

"We have discussed what options are open to us. If you wish to continue to photograph around the club then you will be punished for breaking our agreement." Quentin said sternly.

"P.. p.. punished?" said Maggie questioningly.

Jim took over the conversation. Fixing Maggie with a baleful stare he said:

"It is the decision of the committee that you be soundly spanked. This will serve not only as punishment for your unguarded behaviour but will hopefully impress on you the need for vigilance and be a deterrent against future transgressions."

Maggie looked from one to the other of the four men sitting in judgement on her. Anger pulsed through her body and exploded from her as she spat:

"SPANKED? SPANKED? Why you pompous b......"

Maggie felt a long finger sealing her lips and closing her mouth. Paul's hand grasped her chin and turned her to face him.

"Consider carefully before you respond Maggie. Taking a spanking is a short sharp shock to the system I grant you, but will be over and done with here. Otherwise you face being banned from the club and failing to complete your project. Take a minute to think before you answer."

Maggie stood shaking with emotion, her mouth opening and closing as she tried to sort out what she was thinking. Breathing deeply she acknowledged to herself that there was only one course of action she could possibly take. Her project meant everything to her and she had to safeguard her ability to complete it. What was a spanking anyway? That's what children got for misbehaving. A few swats to her bottom and it would be over. The worst thing about it would be the humiliation she thought. That was likely to stay with her for a long time. Weighing everything up she had to admit it was her own foolish actions which had placed her in this invidious situation so she should just suck it up and get on with it. She would take the spanking for the sake of her art.

She turned back to the committee and said very quietly

"Alright I choose to be s..s..s.." she couldn't bring herself to even say the word "punished".

Jim looked at Maggie and said:

"Maggie you need to be clear about what you are accepting. You will receive 4 dozen spanks on your bare bottom. Once the spanking has commenced you can not change your mind. If you struggle or try to prevent the spanking it will be extended. Do you understand?"

Gasping, as she processed what he had just said she cringed as she repeated to herself, " 4 dozen, 48 spanks." Oh my, this wasn't going to just be a few casual swats and bare bottom! Good grief bare bottom in front of all these men. She couldn't stand that. She couldn't permit someone to do that to her. But what was the alternative, what about the project?

Feeling that she was well and truly stuffed, she shrugged her shoulders and muttered:

"'K"

Jim, trying to control a grin that was itching to escape his iron control, queried

"What was that Maggie?"

She looked up, sending him a look of absolute loathing and spat out the words at him,

"OK!"

Hearing Paul's quiet voice in her ear saying:

"I'd watch that attitude if I were you. Adam has a very strong arm and he doesn't need any more motivation to really wallop you"

Maggie paused, Adam, so this was his role, now she understood what the 'member without portfolio' got to do.

With a nod from Jim, Adam stood up and brought his chair into the centre of the semicircle facing the others. Taking Maggie's shoulders, Paul nudged her forward until she was standing facing Adams' right thigh. Before she had an opportunity to recoil or react in any way Paul slipped down her jeans and panties and Adam flipped her over his lap.

She cried out and struggling, tried to get off until with a very loud 'Thwap' as Adam's hand met her buttocks full force. Maggie screamed as her breath galed from her lungs like a wheezy zephyr. She felt as if her nether region had met a sizeable wooden plank. Stunned into inactivity she steeled herself for the next blow. Adam set off in a steady rhythm. The first slap had been designed to get her attention and prevent her from struggling. It had succeeded in both areas. Now his attention to her buttocks was rewarded with a chorus of 'ows', 'ahhhs', 'ohs', and 'oh no's' interspersed with occasional 'help me, stop him's'. Adam continued relentlessly. He had completed the first dozen when he paused, giving Maggie a rest and to rub a little of the sting out of her reddening cheeks for a few moments. As her breathing calmed he said to her

"Are you ready for the next set Maggie?"

A plaintiff "Yes" could be heard between sniffs and so Adam began again. He wasn't hitting her hard but her virgin bottom had never felt anything like this onslaught before, and she was unprepared for the accumulative effect of the stinging as her punishment proceeded. He concentrated groups of three spanks on alternate cheeks, moving them around the surface of her taut mounds. She became especially vocal with her complaints when he delivered stinging slaps to the tender area where thighs and buttocks meet.

Two dozen completed he continued without a pause. Maggie was becoming more distressed and her attempts to wriggle off his lap were becoming more frenzied. He gripped her waist with his left hand and tucked her firmly against him, quelling her movements.

With every spank, Maggie gasped she tried to relax her buttocks. She had realised that clenching them in anticipation of the next slap only increased the sting. Her bottom was on fire and the sting was unbelievably fierce. She could not believe that Adam could continue to spank so hard and so consistently. She had lost count of how many she had already received but was praying they would be over soon. She hated to be so out of control and was crying more wildly now her legs kicking to try and ease the stinging.

Without noticing that the spanking had ended, Maggie felt gentle hands replacing her clothing as Adam helped her to her feet. Tears were coursing down her cheeks as he held her in a tight hug. Looking over to the committee she said softy

"I'm sorry guys." Which was followed by three pairs of arms hugging her in succession.

As the committee dispersed Paul held on to Maggie cuddling her closely and rubbing her back whilst her tears dried and her breathing returned to normal. He kissed the top of her head lightly and tipping her face up to his he said

"You've had quite a day."

Nodding with a self pitying expression on her face which provoked a shout of laughter from Paul, Maggie voiced her concern.

"Can I really come back for the rest of my shots?"

"Yes but mind I've been given responsibility for ensuring you keep to the conditions of the agreement. So I'm going to be keeping a very close eye on you for as much time as I can manage"

Maggie smiled and said

"I think I'll like that".

The exhibition of student's work was a total success. Maggie's rowing montage centre piece was declared a major triumph whilst displaying a high degree of freshness and innovation. There was a great deal of interest in her work both within and outwith the University and she had the great satisfaction of being asked to exhibit more of her work by the gallery owners.

Continuing to feel an affinity with the rowers, Maggie continued to watch and photograph their races and enjoyed some spectacular end of season parties at the rowing club partnered by Paul. He had, true to his word, kept such a close eye on her that he had virtually moved in to her rooms. They rubbed along extremely harmoniously together and Paul no longer worried about her tendency to become too wrapped up in her art to eat and sleep. He had found a simple whisper of a five letter word beginning with "s" in her ear was enough to ensure immediate compliance.

Stephen P Webb

Spring 2018

A Cottage in the Woods :

Lady Constance was still a good looking woman. "Fair, fat and over forty" was a phrase that came to her, at times, as she stood before her mirror.

It did her less than justice. Her reflection had gazed back as she swivelled her head in search of new lines. Her fingertips traced from chin to throat in a hopeful gesture of smoothing, although all seemed to have survived another night. She had shrugged off her dressing gown to examine herself in the mirror full length. Having not been condemned with large breasts, gravity had been unable to do its worst, and hers still stood quite firm. Still, she had been unable to resist her innate femininity and had arched her back with a quick intake of breath, to remember them again as they had once stood unaided. She cocked her head to one side and let her gaze travel down. The flat belly of youth was now another memory, filling out, as her hips had spread. Still that is what child birth did and she had done her duty, producing the requisite heir and spare and had also provided a bonus daughter for her husband to dote on.

Their marriage had been one ostensibly of politics and convenience. Yet still there was affection between them even though they were more like business partners and good friends, than lovers. There were still times when her husband attended to her in her chambers, although these occasions were becoming infrequent. His attention, although not at all unwelcome and the resulting union, still pleasurable, was but a pale shadow of their wild rutting of youth. Her husband sadly was also not immune to the pacifying nature of time passing.

Yet, sometimes, she needed more, to feel the glorious rapture again

2

The woodsman sat outside his cottage. Built with his own hands from materials he had cut, sawn, begged and, just occasionally, even bought. It seemed to grow from the earth, at one with its surrounding.

Long years in the woods had sharpened his senses, attuned him to the sights and sounds of normality. Someone was coming his way.

Within a few minutes she appeared at first, just the suggestion of colour flitting through the trees.
He paid her no attention when she finally walked into his clearing, busying himself with sorting out his fishing lines and rods.

Elegant and serene, she moved past him with grace, and entered his cottage.

Still he busied himself with his chores, ignoring her as if she had been a passing breeze.

At last he rose, moved inside and carefully replaced his work and tools before turning to her.
She stood with her back to him, her hips pressed against a small table that was one of the few articles of furniture he allowed. He let his gaze travel down from the cascade of chestnut hair that flowed over her shoulders pointing to her still trim waist. A waist that flared out to a fine full bottom, that lead to long tapered legs. Tanned, toned, a picture of pure feminine beauty.

He walked to a firm upright chair and spun it round quietly to face away from the table. Sat down and waited. The suspense mounted. At last, she turned to stand at his right side. Slid her hands down and slowly lifted her dress to bunch it around her waist. He reached for the waist band of her panties and slipping his fingers inside, he eased them down, spreading the waist to minimise contact, for he knew that this is what she preferred. Not bunched, or pulled or any other crass clumsiness, rather to lose her final defence, almost without feeling their loss.

She neither wanted nor needed any unseemly caress or embrace, and simply lowered herself over his lap, offering herself to his tender mercies.

He started firmly from the off. His hand, hardened and strengthened by years of manual labour, contrasted with the soft pillows of her bottom. In a contest, where there could be only one winner.

Varying the pace and target area, he steadily increased the strength until her breath was reduced to quick gasps as her body squirmed, her reddening buttocks tensing and releasing in subconscious reaction.

At last, when even his hard hand had begun to complain, her knees bent and she slid from his lap to squat, panting, beside his chair.

She stood at last and, without a glance, moved to the table, bent over and grasped the opposite edge with whitened finger tips.

He rose and reached for the top section of his fishing rod. Thin, whippy carbon fibre, smooth and immensely strong.

He walked to her side and laid the first six on slowly, giving her time to absorb the sting and raise her bottom for the next. He continued in groups of six, some fast some slow. He varied the angles and intensity as he watched for signs of her surrender, letting her decide when she could take no more.

She was lost in a world of her own, where only the table top, the soft swish of the rod, her hammering heart and the fire in her body existed. Her previously red bottom was now ablaze, each individual line merging to become as one. Her knees buckled again and she slid slowly forwards to the floor, her upper body sliding across his table top arms still outstretched, still elegant and controlled.

He replaced the rod and returned to stand beside her, to be there if she needed support. At long last her breathing calmed and she started to rise.

He returned to the chair, slid down his trousers and underwear and sat down as she walked over.

"Somewhat presumptuous!" she thought. Straddling the chair she lowered herself slowly devouring him inch by inch. Years of horse riding had given her strong legs and an excellent rhythm. The trot became a canter, then full gallop, her breathing grew ragged. As the fence approached she rose to almost disconnection before thrusting down to land hard, squirming and bucking as she bent backwards in ecstasy. During her ride he had freed her breasts from restraint. She pushed forward, crushing their tips against his rough shirt, as she continued her canter. Clamping down her muscles to hold him tight, caressing him, milking him. She felt his moment approach, her back arched, each movement rubbed her aroused nipples against his chest, driving herself upwards again, so that their moment of release clashed in glorious coincidence.

As she fell from her high, the realisation came that his hands, which, during her gyrations, had supported her striped, hot bottom, were still in place. There was even the suggestion of some kneading and caressing! She reached down and eased them away, softening the gesture by allowing him a small smile.

After a few breathless moments she stood up, retrieved her panties, refastened and smoothed down her dress, ran her fingers through her hair in a timeless female gesture, turned and walked out the door.

Not a word had been spoken, required or needed.

He also walked to the door, just in time to see her melt into the trees, and returned to his seat outside the cottage

To await Her Ladyship's Pleasure………….

3

Lady Constance's connection with the Woodsman had endured for many years. Looking back with a wry smile she reflected on their many trysts in his cottage in the woods or around the land of her husband's estate. Their meetings of late had followed a familiar, pleasurable rhythm and had become a routine way to fulfil her need. It had not always been so.

She remembered when the woodsman had first appeared on the estate. She was a new bride learning what her husband expected of her and fulfilling her role in their society. The marriage had been arranged by their fathers in the way of two great companies merging and setting up a new branch of influence in a neighbouring environment.

She had accepted her father's choice of husband if not joyfully, resignedly. She found that he was a kind man, not overly intelligent or blessed with any degree of insight, somewhat pompous and harbouring an inflated conception of his own importance. Traits, she found she could work with or around, as her skills evolved.

Constance had found it easy to convey a greater depth of compliance and pleasure in their union than she had ever felt. She quickly learned to gauge his tolerance levels for irony and teasing, to know when he needed her to appear submissive to his ego in public and to service his libido at night. They had journeyed through the maze of sexual enlightenment together, she, a young virgin, having never spent an hour alone in a man's company prior to marriage, and he with a rather formulaic approach to achieving his own release and little experience in leading a woman on the road toward sexual fulfilment.

Her education had advanced the year the woodsman arrived. He had worked on the old Viscount's estate since he was a lad. He had done well and his skills were very respected. When the Count's son prepared to set up home with his new bride, the woodsman had accepted the position of Estate Manager and had moved into his little cottage in the woods. He played a very active role in the estate where he preferred to work with his hands, to lead his team of groundsmen by example and to share his skills with the younger lads.

In his time off, he enjoyed fly fishing and would spend many happy hours on the miles of river that wound through the estate. It was whilst battling to entice a particularly wily brown trout in the deep water pools beneath the meadow footbridge that he first met Lady Constance. He was aware of her approach long before she noticed him in the water. She was walking barefoot through the wild flower meadow picking bunches of cowslips and primroses and the tiny wild daffodils which clothed the riverbank.

As he watched her she swung her long bare legs over the bank and paddled swirling the water into whirlpools with her toes. The sun was hot but she in her simple cotton dress looked cool and comfortable. Downwind, the Woodsman caught her light perfume as a light dusky musk carried on the gentle breeze. He felt his manhood stirring as he drank in the vision of woman before him. His eyes caressed the swell of her breasts, the soft downy skin of the exposed throat cloaked by drifts of wavy chestnut hair. Her round full lips pursed and relaxed as she sang quietly to herself.

His gaze lingered on the peach like skin of her cheeks which he longed to mumble with his lips. Slowly roaming around her face absorbing the features, colours and textures of her, his eyes sought hers. In an electrifying burst of connectivity his body thrilled as their eyes met. Shocked, but at the same time stunned into inaction they remained joined in visual communication, a link strong and enduring across the river divide.

Appraising his muscular frame, tanned skin and dark black hair, Constance felt the moisture in her mouth evaporate. She drew her tongue around her lips, but her mouth was too dry to hydrate them. She became aware of shallow breathing and felt heat warm her cheeks. She was trapped in his gaze, a captive in his hypnotic beam. Maintaining eye contact, she eased herself into the water. Standing on a shingle shelf, it was not deep, barely reaching to her knees. Her dress skirts swirled around her in the gentle current. Her hands strayed to the button above her breasts. She opened it and gradually moving her hands down the length of her dress she undid them all. She let the dress fall from her shoulders and flicked it onto the river bank.

Reeling in his fly the Woodsman slowly recovered his line without taking his eyes from Constance. He watched her wade out into the central stream of current the water lapping her at mid thigh. Slowly she closed the distance between them whilst her hands worked to unfasten her brassiere. Sensuously she revealed her beautiful breasts. He could see the nipples standing erect and proud, rising and falling rapidly as her chest strove with her now ragged breathing. Crossing to his side of the river she stood at little more than an arms-length from him.

He smiled and touched her cheek, her head turned into his hand and her lips pressed his palm. With his other hand he threw his rod to shore. He touched her cheek again, this time sliding his hand around until it cupped the back of her neck. She went rigid at this attempt to gather her to him and lifted her hand to shove his arm away. He simply closed his fingers over her wrist. She stood there, the breath backing up in her lungs and her pulse throbbing hard and thick.

He wasn't smiling now. He leaned in until his lips were an inch from hers. The kiss hovered there, a breath away until the hand she'd levered against his arm changed its grip. She moved into him.

She didn't think, even for an instant, she wanted to see, wanted to know, wanted to feel.

His mouth was soft, more persuasive than possessive. His lips nibbled hers open so that he could slide his tongue over them, to cloud her senses with flavour. Heat gathered like a fireball in her lungs even before he touched her, those clever hands moulding over the snug fit of cotton over her hips, slipping seductively over her flesh.

With a kind of edgy delight, she felt herself go damp.

It was that mouth that generous and tempting mouth he'd thought he'd wanted. But the moment he'd tasted it, he'd wanted all of her. She was pressed against him her soft slim body beginning to vibrate. Her small firm breast weighed gloriously in his palm and he could hear the passion that sounded in her throat, all but taste it as her mouth moved eagerly on his.

He wanted to forget the patience and control he'd taught himself to live by, and just ravage. Here the violence of need all but erupted inside him. He would have dragged her to the ground if she hadn't struggled back pale and panting.

She put up her hands **"No"** she said, the first word they had exchanged.

"It was wrong of me"

He stepped toward her. If she had stepped back, he would have pursued, like any hunter after the prize. But she faced him squarely, and shook her head. It was a shock to see the effort he expended to regain control to witness fury and frustration wash vividly across his face.

"I'm sorry", she said placing her hand on his chest.

"You need to be." He growled taking hold of her wrist once again. She looked into his face and nodded.

"Make me sorry" she whispered.

His muscular arms swept her up to the river bank depositing her there with some force. He followed and urging her to keep up with him strode to the trunk of an ancient oak tree.

He sat down and making her stand between his legs………….

4. To here

………………., an arm across her breasts in an act of unconscious feminine protection.
He aimed a quick slap at her thigh and she dropped her hands in protection.
"Little late for false modesty Lady, leave your arms down so I can see you clear. T'was not long since you saw fit to flaunt your beauty."

She stood, eyes cast down, fear and excitement fought tumultuous war in her body.

He tipped up her chin with one finger and leant toward her so they were eye to eye.
He spoke with quiet iron, softly, but with a voice that pierced her inner being.
"Think yourself the fine lady? Who can raise a man's passion then cast him aside?
Do you suppose I am to be treated so? Do you consider me a mere chattel, a play thing, to discard after brief amusement?

As he held her eyes he reached down for the hem of her slip. Grabbed a fistful in each hand and slowly drawing his arms apart the fine silk ripped. Her breasts quivering with each shuddering breath, as with agonising slowness the slip split, their eyes still locked. With a final wrench it parted and fluttered to the ground. His fingers caught the waist band of her fine silk knickers and pulled them away before releasing with a snap.
"Down." The single word growled out.
She must remove her final concealment herself! Such sweet agony….
After a brief hesitation she slipped her fingers in the waist band and drew them aside, slipped them down over the firm fullness of her buttocks, let them drop to form a silken pool at her feet.

"Sorry!" she spoke again faintly. He leaned back and let his gaze drink in her full length, the smooth stretch of neck, the ripe firm breasts rising and falling like a gentle wave on a beach with every anxious breath. Her round stomach as yet little touched by the rigours of child birth. The soft mound of her sex resplendent in rich chestnut curls, a beauty indeed. A captivating picture of mature womanhood, still touched with the glow of youth. For a moment his resolve weakened.

She broke the spell with a faint repeat of her earlier plea. "Make me sorry."

"Aye lass, reckon I will."

He swept his right arm down catching her just below her knees and swept her off her feet as if she was a child. His left arm grabbed her shoulder as he dropped her unceremoniously across his lap. "Reckon I will." he repeated with quiet decision.

For so long this desire had lain dormant and unspoken, for so long she had rejected these feeling with thoughts of self recrimination. Had hinted, teased and cajoled her husband without effect. His imagination was too narrow, his experience too limited to respond. Now.......

Still the first blow came as a shock. The power was beyond her early imagination, the sting more than she could bear. Yet she must endure. She was propelled forward so that he was induced to grab her waist and hold her tight against his hips. Her fingers scrabbled at the soft grass as the oaken hand fell again and again. With kicking legs and plaintive cry she became unable to distinguish any particular part as the whole of her soft bottom was set ablaze.

His hand lifted from its tight grip on her waist and she thought, with a confusing mixture of hope and fear that her trial was over. Another slap, more push than blow, slid her forward to pivot over his left knee. His right leg swung round to part her thighs and pinion her flailing left, exposing her fully to his gaze, the soft, sensitive, underside of each hot mould presented for his attention. He began again.

Yet through the pain she noticed the hard lump pressed against her thigh. The realisation brought awareness that her own sex was likewise a throbbing ache. She began to welcome the pain as a mask for it's clarion call.

How long she lay squirming, unaware that he had stopped, she knew not. His strong hand lifted her to her stumbling feet. He held her shoulders until assured she could stand unaided. Then, with a firm "Wait here" he strode away to retrieve her dress.

She turned her lowered gaze to watch as he strode away, the blaze in her rear pleading for her hands. But she was the Lady Constance, she would not allow such comforting. Her conscious mind rejected her arousal, the throb and dampness of her sex made lie to such thoughts.

He returned to deliver her dress as he stooped to lift her slip and knickers. She slipped it on and stumbled over the buttons with trembling hand.

"My cottage" was all he said, neither request nor order, simply a statement of what would be.

She walked swiftly away, not allowing herself the indignity of running, the blaze in her bottom reinforcing the fire in her body. He followed closely behind as befitted his station. Quickly she slipped inside and he followed, turning to fasten the door. As he turned back she had already unfastened the buttons. He took a step towards her as she let her dress slip off once more..................

5

...............................her arms went around him, fingers diving into his hair. Her body slammed into his, vibrating as his mouth captured hers and the kiss grew rough, then brutal. His mouth was hot, almost vicious. The shock of it sent flares of reaction straight to her centre. The wind had been knocked out of her by the suddenness, and the rage under it, and the shock of need that slammed into her like a fist.

It was quick seconds only, before her mouth was free.

"Stop it" she demanded, and hated that her voice was only a shaky whisper.

"Whatever you think," he began, struggling for his own composure, "there are times when you need someone. Right now, it's me." Impatience shimmering around him he waited for her to decide.

The seconds ticked by lasting a millennium of indecision. Constance' eyes roamed his form a wave of pleasure rippling through her when she heard his breath catch as her gaze met his. In less than a heartbeat she was in his arms, wild, reckless energy was bursting inside her. She couldn't move quickly enough, her hands were not fast enough to satisfy the craving as she wrenched him from his clothes.

His arm was beneath her knees sinking with her in front of the dull embers of the banked fire. The moment they were prone on the floor she would have straddled him her need for release driving and fierce but he flipped their positions, muffling her protests with his hard searching mouth.

She snatched her swollen mouth free "I want you inside me."

"You only want one aspect inside you" he murmured.

"Goddamn it," She began, then groaned when he dipped his head and took her breast in his mouth. She was lost in sensations barely comprehended.

Sex for her with her husband had always been quick, simple and satisfied a basic need. But this was tangling of emotions, a war on the system, a battering of the senses.

She writhed against him struggling to get her hand between them, to reach him where he lay hard and heavy against her. Pure panic set in when he braceleted her wrists and levered her hands over her head.

"Don't"

He'd nearly released her in reflex before he saw her eyes. Panic yes, even fear, but desire too. "You can't always be in control, My Lady."

He caressed her sensitive skin, tracing his fingers up toward the heat, then back again. Her breath was coming in pants now as she fought to roll away from him.

"You want the kick without the intimacy. You don't need a partner for that and today you have one. I'm going to give as much pleasure as I get."

Looking back with the indulgence of memory Constance smiled as she recalled that first encounter and her initiation as a sensual being. He was the architect of her enlightenment. Even through the haze of years she could feel that moment when her body imploded. One moment the tension was vicious, then the spear of pleasure arrowed into her, so sharp, so hot. He had driven her to climax again, this time ripping through her like claws and an eon later as their bodies lay quiet and meshed together he had slipped gently inside her again.

She watched him, incapable of resisting the fresh onslaught of pleasure. He kept the rhythm slow now, with long deep stokes that stirred the soul. All she could process was that lovely fluid slide of his body in hers, the tireless friction of it that had yet another orgasm shivering through her like gold. She had experienced orgasm before but always equated it with a subtle pop of a cork from a bottle of stress, not the violent explosion that destroyed a lifetime of restraint.

As her mind journeyed back she placed her hands on her still firm bottom cheeks and nodded ruefully, smiling at the irony that the fire lit that perfect day by the riverbank had continued to smoulder and burn throughout these many years. Flaring up with insistent need, demanding to be fed, stoked and then left burning brightly for some time before dampening down and cooling before flaring once again.

Constance and the woodman had tended the fire. Early on with novel fuel stacking it high and tending it often but gradually over the years they had learned what was needful and settled into that rhythm as effortlessly as breathing.

Stephen P Webb - Spring 2018

The Antique Shop :

They were coming to the end of the long row of boxes labelled as mixed lots for the auction commencing at 2pm. There was nothing but piles of old chipped china and glassware as far as she could see, certainly nothing to excite the degree of interest already expended. Lucy was restless and wanted to move on. This was supposed to be her afternoon off and her idea of a relaxed perusing of the shops did not include dusty crowded auction rooms.

She had tried to be patient as she realised this was important to her friend and he was engrossed in scanning the boxes and ferreting out potential bargains and was plainly enjoying himself to a degree she simply could not comprehend. He had so much junk already in his modern little flat – how could he contemplate adding yet more!

She sighed deeply and wishing to get his attention, she turned to face him as he wandered between the lots noting items of interest in his catalogue.

"Can we go now? Please" she looked into his face giving what she fondly imagined was an impression of Penelope, that saintly and patient companion of legend.

"Yes ok," he said aware that she had been restless for a while, "There is nothing I'm desperate to bid on just now,"

"You don't say" She muttered under her breath rolling her eyes heavenward in a gesture far from any described in Homer but redolent of an impatient and rather self-absorbed modern woman.

Angus reached for her hand and led her out of the fusty auction room and into the light and warmth of an autumn day. He was aware of feeling a tad irked by her attitude, something he had tasked her about on more than one occasion. It seemed his advice had not been taken and one day soon he would need to take a hand in adjusting that attitude for her. However he put this to one side as they window shopped along the high street of this ancient town.

Down one of the cobbled alleyways covered in tubs of vibrant autumn flowering crocuses, Angus spotted a small sign, almost hidden by the remains of the colourful hanging baskets of summer -

"Edwards Antiquities – by private appointment only". Being a confident, calm and assured man he suggested they walk up the narrow alley and 'just see' if they could call ad hoc.

Shrugging her shoulders with a resigned air Lucy agreed – she secretly enjoyed looking in antique shops loving the feel and patina of old wood and the sense that objects were waiting, cloaked in the history of their previous owners, to begin the next chapter of their story. These romantic fancies imbued many of the objects with mystery adding to their charm and value for her.

As they approached the old stone building it did not look like a shop at all, but just like someone's home. Angus knocked and a man answered. He was old, late 70s perhaps – but tall of stature and with sharp alert eyes. This was Mr Edwards. Angus and he discussed a viewing and Lucy was delighted the men seemed to have struck a chord as they were invited into his shop.

It was full of wonderful things, furniture and paintings – but arranged naturally room by room so it looked just like a home. The only difference being little cards and labels were attached to many of the objects on display. Mr Edwards offered tea – an offer gratefully accepted and he disappeared while the curious pair began exploring.

Besides lovingly stroking items of furniture, revelling in the colours and textures of the old woods, Lucy loved the 'little things' – button hooks, old kitchen implements, little jewellery boxes, and glass wear. All, as you would expect, showing varying signs of ageing, testimony to their having been a part of busy working lives – but the condition and quality were excellent. Angus was already making a small collection of things he had found and wanted.

It was whilst admiring some intricate marquetry on the back board of a Victorian wash stand that Lucy spotted an exquisitely made hair brush. The wood of the handle and back were Oak with delightfully delicate pearl and shell inlays, shining and smooth under a matt lacquer finish. She looked at the label, 'Made in 1824'. Studying the brush she frowned, puzzled as she contemplated the chance of that label being correct. Surely it was a mistake, the bristles looked immaculate – like new? She picked it up and paused, it was a lovely object, wonderful to hold.

She took it over to show Angus and also to ask Mr Edwards if the year was correct. As she gave it to Angus he was equally struck by the beauty of the workmanship and how perfectly it felt to hold. It was like it belonged in his hand.

"Ah!" said Mr Edwards "that is indeed a very old brush, a Bromley & Overton brush, brush-makers to royalty, a very popular wedding gift amongst the aristocracy in those days."

"But it looks unused, as if new with all the bristles still perfect. How could it have survived like this?" Lucy queried.

Mr Edwards looked at her in a knowing way. "Well, my dear, a brush has ….other uses. If you care to look at your companion…… look how he is holding the brush."

They all looked. Unconsciously, Angus had found the most comfortable way to hold the brush – and they saw that he was holding it backwards.

"He is holding it correctly, just as I have done for nearly 40 years, right up to the time my dear wife, Cecelia, passed over. It was her brush, presented to her by her own mother on our wedding day." He paused. "But we were never able to have children… so it now seeks a new home…"

Lucy was puzzling over this, it was Cecelia's brush but Mr Edwards 'held it'?

Angus on the other hand had immediately understood the true purpose of the brush. There was a silent but manly exchange of approving glances as Angus slowly withdrew his gaze and fixed it on Lucy's face. He could see she was still perplexed as to what Mr Edwards was alluding to. The feel of the brush, its comfortable weight in his hand, had given Angus an idea, confirmed rather, something he had been leading up to. Perhaps this visit to the Antique Shop was destined to trigger a change in the way he managed his relationship with his little impatient firebrand.

"Forty years of marriage – a wonderful achievement, what was the secret to remaining happily married for all that time?" Angus asked the shop keeper.

"Well, I can only say the brush helped us both and if you do not mind me saying, my wife's bottom was most glorious to spank, right to the end. My Cecelia was 'aglow' to her final days."

Mr Edwards looked at Lucy who was now wide-eyed and blushing. "You remind me a lot of her – if I may say." Lucy felt two pairs of male eyes focus on the curves of her hips and bottom but before she could express the growing sense of outrage she felt stirring, she heard Angus asking,

"How much is the brush?"

"I could not part with it for money" said Mr Edwards "… but I do want it to go to a good home… a loving home…a spanking home… and if I knew that were to be so – I would bestow it as a gift, just as I received it"

There was a pause.

"Would you two like some privacy… to discuss matters?" Mr Edwards asked Angus, aware of the mutinous, outraged expression on the petite woman's face. "My study, perhaps?" another pause, "I'll go and make some tea – but I won't hurry…"

Mr Edwards disappeared to the kitchen.

Looking back, he saw Angus take Lucy by the hand and lead her quite determinedly into the study. Oh, the expression on Lucy's face was a picture. He could not help but smile.

He took his time. Tea, earl grey, a mix of cakes and biscuits… freshly made Lemonade. He prepared the tray and walked slowly back towards the front parlour, stopping outside the study door.

There was a sound, a familiar sound, the crisp brisk sound of a spanking in progress. Nothing, to him, was quite so arousing as the sound of the brush kissing the bared upturned cheeks of a deserving bottom accompanied as in this case by the moans and cries of the recipient. Unashamedly listening at the door Mr Edwards could hear the sound of a relationship being redefined, of rules being established and the air cleared between two people who were coming to a mutual understanding.

"Oh Angus, oooooooh ….. ahhhhhhh ………oh my bottom ……. ooooooowwwww……..I will be good…… promise I will………oh god… ooooooooohhhh." Lucy's voice bleated as she was introduced to a very different aspect of her lover's character. Gone was the tolerant and placid man she was always able to best in an argument, replaced by a determined dominant whose scolding was ringing in her ears just as the brush was paddling her bare, now crimson, bottom.

Could Mr Edwards have seen through the closed door of the study, his eyes would have found Lucy, her skirt about her waist, her silky, lacy panties at her knees, over Angus's lap as he delivered a sound spanking, her bottom becoming ever redder and more tender.

"Stop Angus, please stop." Lucy tried in vain to protect her bottom by reaching back with her hands only to feel them expertly caught and braceletted by Angus's large strong hands.

He laid the brush down on the desk beside him and adjusted the position of the wriggling bottom before him. Without pausing he continued the lesson he hoped to teach using the flat of his hands to deliver a volley of unremittingly hard spanks across the entire area. The sounds of mounting distress from Lucy had him pause and rub the beleaguered bottom gently, kneading it and soothing the angry looking cheeks. He had never spanked anyone as hard as he had spanked her this day and smiled to himself as he heard the torrent of apologies and assurances of improved behaviour to come.

He slowly released Lucy's hands and helped her to her feet. As she stood in front of him her eyes glistening with unshed tears Angus drew her closer to him and embraced her, rubbing her back to soothe her whilst she recovered her equilibrium and her breathing restored to normal rhythm. As she slowly regained her senses Lucy stiffened and began to withdraw from Angus's circling arms, she felt extremely embarrassed and ……. Sore! She'd never been treated in such a way before and she could not unravel the complex rush of emotions and thoughts that beset her. All she knew is that she wanted to get away from everyone.

As she took a step back Angus stood refusing to let her detach from him. She began to shrug her shoulders meaning to leave immediately but he wouldn't relinquish his hold. She looked up at him and said in a wobbly voice "Leave me alone Angus"

He looked closely at her and seeing her confusion and embarrassment he smiled, "Not in this lifetime," he said, and taking her firmly by the hand he opened the door to the study and strode into the shop.

Mr Edwards was just tying off the string of the parcel containing Angus's purchases when he heard them enter the room. Glancing over he summed the situation up in a heartbeat and rose to his feet offering the parcel to Angus and opening the front door for them to pass through. They left with a grateful nod of acknowledgement from Angus and a shamefaced smile from his lady.

Closing the door with a rueful smile Mr Edwards locked up for the day and headed, with the untouched tea tray, into his office looking around and breathing deeply as the flood of poignant memories comforted and consoled him. He hoped he'd see more of that young couple in the future.

Stephen P. Webb - Spring 2018

Printed in Great Britain
by Amazon